# WHAT READERS ARE SAYING ABOUT THE HORSES OF HALF MOON RANCH:

"An exciting and page-turning book, perfect for horse lovers."

"A thrilling start to Horses of Half Moon Ranch. I would recommend anyone who is able to read it to do so."

"I couldn't put this book down!"

"An exciting and gripping read."

"This is the best book I have ever read. Jenny Oldfield's whole series is amazing…This story is so well described I would recommend it to all horse lovers."

"I totally love the Half Moon Ranch series by Jenny Oldfield. I've read nearly all of them and I can never put them down until I've finished them, they're so good."

"This story is one that I enjoyed. I hope that the author will continue to display such talent in writing."

"I found this book really thrilling and couldn't put it down."

"This is a good read for any horse lover. I enjoyed it a lot."

"You can fall in love with the adventurous story line, and get flown away to the Western U.S., where you will meet galloping horses under starlight. Gives the reader an interesting, always-on-the-move, adventurous, story line."

"I found this book very moving…I highly recommend [it]."

"Another great book by Jenny Oldfield."

"The best. I felt that I was there."

"Brilliant! I loved this book."

"I would recommend to any horse lover!"

The Horses of

# HALF MOON RANCH

# *Crazy Horse*

*The Horses of*

# HALF MOON RANCH

by Jenny Oldfield
Wild Horses
Rodeo Rocky
Crazy Horse
Johnny Mohawk
Midnight Lady
Third-Time Lucky

The Horses of

# HALF MOON RANCH

# *Crazy Horse*

Jenny Oldfield

Published by Sourcebooks Jabberwocky, an imprint of Sourcebooks, Inc.
P.O. Box 4410, Naperville, Illinois 60567-4410
(630) 961-3900
Fax: (630) 961-2168
www.sourcebooks.com

Originally published in Great Britain in 1999 by Hodder Children's Books.

Library of Congress Cataloging-in-Publication Data

Oldfield, Jenny.
    Crazy Horse / Jenny Oldfield.
        p. cm. — (Horses of Half-Moon Ranch ; bk. 3)
    Summary: When Crazy Horse and Cadillac, two very different but inseparable horses, go missing from the Half-Moon Ranch in Colorado, thirteen-year-old Kirstie tries to recover the stolen animals.
    [1. Horses—Fiction. 2. Ranch life—Colorado—Fiction. 3. Stealing—Fiction. 4. Colorado—Fiction.] I. Title.
    PZ7.O4537Cr 2009
    [Fic]—dc22
                                2008039729

Printed and bound in the United States of America.
VP 10 9 8 7 6 5 4 3 2 1

**1**

"This is a game called Hide the Flag!" Matt Scott announced to the group of breathless riders who had followed him and Crazy Horse up the steep mountain slope to Hummingbird Rock.

Close to the edge of the sheer drop into the valley below, Kirstie reined in her horse, Lucky, and turned to grin at her best friend, Lisa Goodman on the gray. "Ready to play?"

"Sure." Lisa drew level on Cadillac, the big gelding she was riding for the day; his creamy white coat shone in the afternoon light. "What do we have to do?"

"See the red bandana in Matt's hand? That's the flag. One team hides it and tries to defend it while the other team tracks it down."

"Hide and seek on horseback." Lisa's shrug showed that she understood. "No problem."

"Don't be too sure." Kirstie's grin broadened.

"Meaning?"

Before Kirstie could answer, her brother, Matt, had begun to split the group of a dozen horses and their riders into two groups. "Charlie, you and Rodeo Rocky head up one team. Crazy Horse and me, we'll take the others." Quickly, he split the dude-ranch guests between himself and the young, dark-haired wrangler.

"How about me?" Lisa called across the bare, granite rock. The cold wind blew her bright auburn curls in a halo around her face.

"You're with me and Crazy Horse!" Matt yelled back, fixing his gray Stetson more firmly on his forehead.

"OK, Lucky, that means you and me end up with Charlie," Kirstie told her palomino, who was only too happy to team up with Rocky, his favorite companion.

"We hide, you seek!" Matt went on organizing the group of bemused visitors. This was the last day of their vacation riding the rugged mountain trails winding out of the green valley slopes of Half Moon Ranch. Tomorrow they would go back home to their closed-in, fume-choked city jobs, and Kirstie's brother was keen to give them a final open-air experience to remember.

So he rode Crazy Horse from the ledge of Hummingbird Rock onto the softer ground where ponderosa pines grew tall and straight and aspen trees shook their flame-red autumn leaves in the breeze. He called his team to follow.

"So how come you think I've got a problem?" Lisa insisted on an answer from Kirstie. She held Cadillac on a tight rein so that his handsome white face was raised high, nostrils flared, ears flicking impatiently.

"Did I say that?" Kirstie opened her gray eyes wide.

"Ye-ah!" Lisa's arms jerked forward as Cadillac suddenly ducked his head. She shot out of her saddle and fell against his strong neck.

"Hmm." Kirstie's lips quivered. "Don't let Cadillac see the bandana!" she warned.

Lisa regained her balance and squirmed back

into the saddle. Immediately, Cadillac began to prance sideways, swishing his tail and shaking his head. "Why not?"

Another grin broke out on Kirstie's tanned face. "Let's just say Hide the Flag is not exactly Cadillac's favorite game!"

"Git on!" Lisa urged her pedigree horse to join the rough-and-tumble fun.

Her team raced across a hundred feet of open ground toward a stand of pine trees along a ridge. Charlie's team followed as he led the charge on Rodeo Rocky. The sorrel shot up the slope, his black mane and tail streaming in the wind.

Cadillac stood stock-still, watching them go.

"C'mon, Cadillac, let's move!" Lisa gave him a kick.

The gray horse turned his head and snorted. He didn't move a muscle.

"Y'all spread out!" Charlie yelled instructions to his team.

The bunched riders fanned out as they reached the trees where Matt's team waited, ready to defend the hidden red flag.

Alert in her saddle, ready to head off a visitor

4

called June Halverson, who was riding Yukon, a brown and white, six-year-old paint, Kirstie sympathized with Lisa's predicament. When Cadillac took it into his head not to join in…well, wild horses wouldn't drag him!

"Hey, git on!" Lisa flicked her switch against the big gelding's round, solid rump. Not a flicker of movement from the bored horse. He stood eyes half-closed, a disdainful look on his aristocratic face.

Meanwhile, Kirstie rode Lucky across Yukon's path to pull June Halverson away from the nook in the pine tree where the flag was hidden.

"Yee-hah!" Matt cried, racing Crazy Horse around the back of the trees and galloping from the side to scatter Charlie's team. His horse tore through low, spiky bushes and brushed the bottom branches of the frail aspens, showering leaves and churning up the soft ground. He slid to a halt in a cloud of dust.

"Over there!" Charlie took a guess and pointed to where he thought the bandana might be hidden. He and Rocky set off at a lope, weaving through the tall, scaly trunks of the pine trees.

"Warm!" Kirstie said to herself, kicking Lucky

into action and following Charlie. Matt, too, spun Crazy Horse around on the spot and charged after the wrangler.

"*C'mon,* Cadillac!" a thin voice wailed from down below.

The beautiful pedigree horse kept all four feet firmly planted. He looked down his long nose at the antics of the rest.

On the ridge, Matt ducked low in the saddle to avoid a branch as Crazy Horse swerved between trees. He cut off Charlie and Rocky just in time. Another few feet and they would have spotted the bandana. Crazy Horse skidded to another spectacular halt, turned, and charged back into the fray.

"That horse sure lives up to his name!" June Halverson gasped at Matt's pale tan mount. Crazy Horse was throwing himself about, spinning, backing up, and racing again as if his life depended on defending the flag.

Kirstie grinned and nodded. She caught her breath, then urged Lucky on again. "Warm!" she whispered as another guest began to circle the right tree. "Hot!" Galloping to intercept, she cut across Matt's path, feeling the shudder from

Crazy Horse's thundering hooves as they hit the soft ground.

Too late! Pat Baker, the guest who was riding Jitterbug, had spotted the red kerchief. He stood in his saddle to reach it, yelling to Charlie and the gang. Every rider reined in his horse and closed in on the spot. Not even Crazy Horse, who came flying to the front, was quick enough to stop the dentist from Denver from seizing the flag to win the game.

"Poor Lisa!" Kirstie sat close to the fire, watching flames lick around the logs and shoot orange sparks into the black sky. Saturday night, late October. Winter was on its way.

"Poor Lisa, nothing!" Her friend had sulked her way through supper, turning her back on the bonfire and staring into the fast-running water of Five Mile Creek.

"I mean it."

"You knew that no way was Cadillac gonna play the stupid game!"

"So what was I supposed to do?" Kirstie tried to bring Lisa around. "That's the way Cadillac is.

He's three parts Thoroughbred and one part mustang, which accounts for him being moody and stubborn, I guess."

"Moody!" Lisa was still disgruntled at being made to look like a fool. "I thought he was an ex–mounted police horse. Didn't the army train him to do as he was told?"

"*Ex*–mounted police horse!" Kirstie emphasized the first syllable, raised her eyebrows, and shrugged. "Mom bought him for Matt when we first came to the ranch five years back. The army couldn't use him because he didn't like joining in marches and stuff with the other horses. They said he was too much of an individual to make a good team player."

"Now you tell me!"

"So anyhow, Matt saw him at the sale barn and, zap, love at first sight!" Kirstie remembered the occasion with a warm glow. Her brother had been fifteen years old—two years older than she was now. Their family had just split up. Their father had left their Denver home, and a few months later, she and her brother had come with their mom to Half Moon Ranch to start a new life with their grandparents. Matt, never one to talk much, had spent most of the first weeks in gloomy silence. He had grudgingly gone along to the horse sale, but the moment he saw Cadillac, his eyes lit up. And that was it: the beginning of a beautiful friendship. Even now, when he was away at college during the week, Matt would regularly call home to check up on his favorite horse.

She glanced across at him now, deep in conversation with Charlie Miller, firelight flickering across their serious faces. "That's where we bought Crazy Horse, too; at the same sale barn. Mom said if we were taking a risk and buying a real beauty with a possible temperament problem, like Cadillac, what we needed to go along with him was a horse we could rely on. He didn't have to be good-looking, just dependable."

She smiled as she pictured Crazy Horse. Where Cadillac's head was long and fine, Crazy Horse's was solid and round. His eyes and ears were large, almost mule-like. With a pale tan coat and sturdy legs, no one in their wildest dreams would call him a handsome horse…

"Dependable?" Lisa echoed with a note of disbelief. In this mood, she seemed to want to disagree with everything Kirstie said. "You think those sliding stops and spins of his make him a safe ride?"

Kirstie frowned and stood up. "Have another hamburger?"

"No…thanks. I mean, no way could anyone except Matt have handled Crazy Horse, the nutty way he acted today."

"Sure they could! Crazy Horse was having a good time out there, that's all!" One more criticism, and she and Lisa would be in deep trouble. Kirstie had to bite her tongue and set off for the barbecue. She was irritated to find that she was being followed. "Cadillac might not like playing Hide the Flag, but Crazy Horse sure does!"

"You got one thing right," Lisa said, beginning to veer off across the grass toward the yard. She'd spotted her mother's pickup truck pulling up outside the ranch house, ready to collect her and drive her into town.

"Yeah, what was that?" *Don't tell me!* Kirstie said to herself. *I don't wanna know!*

"That day at the sale barn, your mom figured the second horse didn't need the looks…"

"Yeah?"

Lisa gave a short, empty laugh. "Like I say, you got that right!"

That was it! Kirstie's temper flared. She strode in front of her departing friend. "So you're saying, not only is Crazy Horse nutty, but there's also a problem with the way he looks?"

"You said it, not me!" Lisa walked on into the cold, dark yard. Across the creek, the horses of Half Moon Ranch had gathered by the white fence of Red Fox Meadow. Shadowy shapes, they stood motionless and watchful.

"No!" Kirstie countered. "You're twisting things. It's you who's got a thing against the horse. If you've got something to say, come right out and say it!"

"OK." Lisa stopped and turned. "The way I see it, your mom was new to the dude-ranch business at the time, and she made a whole heap of mistakes the day she bought those two horses. Number one, Cadillac looks good but he won't do a thing you tell him. Number two, Crazy Horse is just that: crazy!"

"And?" Kirstie invited her to spill everything. She might never talk to Lisa again, but at least she would know exactly what she thought.

Lisa drew herself up and took a deep breath.

"And three, think about it, look at him next time you get a chance. His head's too big, his legs are too short. Honestly, Kirstie, Crazy Horse has to be the ugliest animal around!"

The mood around the fire was relaxed and friendly. Sandy Scott chatted with June Halverson about the history of the quarter horse, a specialist breed begun in the 1930s specifically to work the Rocky Mountain ranches of Colorado, Wyoming, and Montana. Hadley Crane, chief wrangler on the ranch, was playing the mouth organ for June's two young children, Robert and Alice, while Matt and Charlie sat back from the fire's bright glow and continued their earnest conversation.

For a while, Kirstie found it impossible to join in. An argument with Lisa was rare. The two girls had been friends since Kirstie's first day at San Luis Middle School, and they had exchanged friendship bracelets every spring since then. Yet they were as different as night and day, Kirstie realized. With her red hair and bubbly, outgoing personality, Lisa was a town girl who dreamed of moving to the city. Kirstie was fair-haired and quiet. Always dressed in shirt and jeans, she loved the outdoors life and didn't give a darn about her appearance, whereas Lisa, she noticed, had begun to wear makeup and to look in mirrors.

And yet, they did have one vital thing in common. Lisa's dad had left home, too.

*And she likes horses,* Kirstie reminded herself as she sat on the bench beside Hadley. *Or I thought she did, until today.*

"Hey, honey!" Sandy said quietly as she passed by. Her hair, a few shades of blonde darker than Kirstie's, was tucked into the collar of her warm corduroy jacket, her hand wrapped around a mug of hot coffee.

The group was breaking up after the cookout. June took her kids off to bed, ready for the journey home the next day. Pat Baker and his wife shook Hadley's hand and thanked him for organizing a week of excellent trail-riding. The head wrangler nodded briefly and slipped his harmonica into his shirt pocket.

"Charlie!" Hadley called across to his junior wrangler. "Quit fooling around. I got a whole heap of things for you to do!"

Charlie swung his leg over the fence where he was perched and jumped down. He strode over, still in his leather chaps and dusty boots. "Who's fooling around?" he protested with a wink at Kirstie. "I've just been talking to Matt here."

"Yeah, yeah. Young guys like you can talk and talk. It don't get no chores done."

Charlie tipped his hat back on his head. "I've done the chores, Hadley. Tack's all cleaned, horse blankets brushed, yard raked, feeding stalls hosed down…"

The old man raised a hand. "Then I'd get me some sleep if I was you, Charlie. You gotta be up early tomorrow."

"How come? Tomorrow's Sunday."

Until now, Kirstie had only half-listened to the old wrangler's grumbling. She'd been looking at Matt, who'd stayed where he was on the fence, staring up at the stars. But now she tuned in to the plans for next day.

"Yep, but I need you to be up at five, bringing horses in from the remuda and saddling them up, ready for a day out at Lazy B."

"What for?" Charlie was puzzled at the unusual order to work on his day off.

"I promised Jim Mullins we'd be over to help on the roundup." Hadley was already walking away, heading for the bunkhouse where he and Charlie had quarters.

"Roundup?" Forgetting about her quarrel with Lisa, Kirstie jumped up to follow him. A day of riding out on Lazy B's 20,000 acres to bring in the red Hereford cattle for the winter appealed to her sense of adventure. "Can I come?"

"Sure." Hadley nodded and walked on.

"Hey, Matt, you coming on the roundup?" Charlie called.

"No, he's not." Sandy Scott stepped in smartly as she covered the embers of the dying fire with dirt. "Matt has exams next week. He has to stay home and study."

"Yeah, yeah!" Matt jumped down from the fence. "Like I'm ten years old, Mom!"

Satisfied that the fire was dead, Sandy pulled up her coat collar and shrugged. "Sorry."

"I already studied."

"When?"

"Every night last week. I figure I know enough to get by." In front of Charlie, Matt wanted his own way. "Honest, Mom, the best plan is to clear my head with a day out at Lazy B. That way, I'll be rid of all the stress, ready for the tests when I get to Denver tomorrow night."

Face to face with her son, looking up at his six feet two inches, Sandy Scott gave in. "OK, you know best." She turned to confirm with Hadley that both Kirstie and Matt would be joining them on the roundup. "But count me out," she told him with a touch of weariness. "I have to drive the minibus to the airport, drop some people off."

"Sure." Hadley took his orders and disappeared.

Soon, Charlie followed him. Matt stayed by the creek for a few moments, watching Sandy walk slowly toward the ranch across the empty yard. The door of the log-built house swung open, and a light went on in the kitchen. "Will you leave Lucky behind tomorrow and ride Crazy Horse for me?" he asked Kirstie. "He needs to work off some excess energy."

"Sure." She nodded. "Will you take Cadillac?"

It was a question that didn't need an answer. Cadillac and Crazy Horse. Matt's two horses. Beauty and the Beast. Sometimes, Kirstie thought they

16

were all he cared about: his gray pedigree and his ugly, light brown quarter horse.

**2**

There was new snow next morning on Eagle's Peak. Kirstie got out of bed, drew back the drapes, and saw the granite mountain glinting white against the pink dawn sky.

Eagle's Peak, Miners' Ridge, Bear Hunt Rock; they all overlooked the valley where Half Moon Ranch nestled in one of the small pastures that ran like green jewels strung along the silver necklace of Five Mile Creek.

But there was no time to stay at the window and admire the view, Kirstie realized. Charlie was already hard at work in the corral, saddling his own horse, Rodeo Rocky, and brushing down Moose, the sturdy, gray quarter horse who was to be Hadley's mount for the day. Beyond the corral was the creek, and beyond that the frost-covered meadow where Matt was cutting out Cadillac and Crazy Horse from the rest of the herd.

Quickly, Kirstie climbed into her jeans and shirt, pulling on a thick blue sweatshirt and two layers of socks. By the time she glanced out of the window once more, her brother was already leading the ill-matched horses across the wooden footbridge into the corral.

"Breakfast!" Sandy Scott reminded her as she shot downstairs and into the kitchen.

Kirstie grabbed her boots from under the table where she'd kicked them off the previous night. "No time!"

"Sure you have time," her mom insisted. She pushed a stack of waffles covered in a thick layer of maple syrup in her direction. "And eggs!" Crossing to the stove, she got to work on a cooked meal that would see Kirstie through the hard day at Lazy B.

"Not hungry," Kirstie protested, stuffing waffle into her mouth.

"Where did I hear that before?" Sandy smiled as she delivered the plate of eggs to the table and eyed the vanishing waffles. "Could it be from Matt, by any chance?"

"Did he have breakfast already?"

"No, he skipped it." Kirstie's mom's smile faded, and she sighed.

"No big deal, Mom. It's only breakfast. I figure he'll survive." Gulping down the eggs, Kirstie showed she was ready to leave.

"Only breakfast," Sandy echoed with a shake of her head. "If only…"

Heading for the porch, Kirstie hesitated. "You worried about Matt for some reason?"

"A little, I guess. He's moody."

So what was new? Kirstie's brother often went into sulks over his lack of social life, the traveling to and from Denver, or some small problem with his girlfriend, Lachelle. "That's Matt."

"But yesterday, before the trail ride, something happened, and he went crazy over it." Sandy had followed Kirstie to the door and stood looking thoughtfully at her son as he saddled Cadillac in the corral. "It was just a phone call from Wes Logan at Ponderosa Pines. You know, the well-heeled guy from California who bought the ranch a couple of years back? He's looking for a horse for his wife, Nancy, and thought we might like to sell Cadillac."

Kirstie swung around. "No way!" was her immediate response.

"That's what I told Mr. Logan. The horse isn't for sale. I softened it a bit—said Cadillac was a little hard to handle. His wife would probably prefer a more docile mount. But when I got off the phone, Matt wouldn't let it drop. He said my 'no' had sounded like 'maybe,' that I wasn't tough enough, and never in a million years would he agree to part with the horse."

Taking her baseball cap from the hook on the porch, Kirstie jammed it firmly onto her head. "Matt overreacted, that's all. Blame it on exam nerves."

"Yeah." Sandy sighed again, then gave a small smile. "I guess I just worry about your older brother."

"Well, don't!" Kirstie leaned across to give Sandy a kiss on the cheek. Outside in the corral, she saw

Hadley mount Moose, ready to set off for Lazy B. "Matt's a big boy. He can take care of himself!"

Sunday was a good day to ride the trails; and the last Sunday in October, when the year's final visitors to Half Moon Ranch were heading for home was the best of all, according to Kirstie.

Meltwater Trail—which took them along the sides of rushing creeks to Miners' Ridge through Dead Man's Canyon—was deserted, just the way she liked it. A red-tailed hawk soared up from a treetop as they passed by a stand of lodgepole pines. A bull elk stood in a clearing of long, dry grass, raised his head, and gave his bugling call, sending two racoons and a family of red foxes scuttling across the trail.

Crazy Horse saw the foxes out of the corner of his eye and skittered sideways. Kirstie reined him to the left, back on course, chiding him for being chicken. "Tiny, tiny foxes!" she told him. "And you, a great big, hulking thing with iron shoes!"

The light brown horse snorted and blew. Up ahead, Hadley reached the end of Miners' Ridge and brought Moose to a halt.

"I fixed on meeting up with Jim Mullins in the next valley," he told Charlie, Kirstie, and Matt. "Four cows holed themselves up there the day before yesterday. We'll round 'em up and head them back to Lazy B by midday."

As the others nodded their agreement, Hadley set Moose off down the slippery descent toward Horseshoe Creek: a thirty-minute trek through more pines and aspens. Reaching the bottom, the four riders let their horses wade into the creek to drink and were greeted by the stocky figure of Jim Mullins astride Monty, his blue roan gelding. Monty's bridle clinked and Jim's polished leather saddle creaked as the rancher approached.

"Any sign of them four runaways?" he asked, turning straight to business. Only a nod in their direction before he cast his gaze up the hillside, the way they'd come.

"Nope." Hadley was like Jim; he never used two words where one would do.

"OK, we spread out and sweep the hill. Don't go too high. It gets kind of vertical up there."

Kirstie glanced up at the ravines littered with fallen trees, at the thick forests and the tiny green clearings. Then she grinned at Charlie. "Kind of like a needle in a haystack!"

"Only the haystack covers 30,000 acres!" he agreed before he and Rodeo Rocky split off and made their way downstream.

She watched Matt rein Cadillac to the left, taking off in the opposite direction of Charlie. Hadley and Moose were retracing their steps the way they'd just come.

"You're with me," Jim told Kirstie, taking her and Crazy Horse up the opposite bank. For a moment, her horse hesitated, turning to stare upriver at Matt and Cadillac wading knee-deep through the creek. The gray horse glanced over his shoulder for a similar check, wanting to establish where his partner was headed. Crazy Horse whinnied, then went on up the hill after Monty.

"Good boy!" Kirstie clicked her tongue and felt him begin the climb, surefooted and steady. *I wish Lisa could see you now!* she said to herself. *Who did she think she was calling crazy?*

Crazy Horse planted each foot firmly on the soft ground, choosing the easiest path between boulders and bushes, not following Monty, whose tactic was simply to bulldoze whatever plant life stood in his way. The rancher's strong quarter horse made rapid, unselective progress, whereas Kirstie's mount was more thoughtful and considerate.

"You're taking good care of me," she murmured gratefully, winding her way to a height some 500 feet above Horseshoe Creek, where they came to a plateau of grassland and, to her surprise, to the four cows they were seeking.

Immediately, as he spotted them browsing through the meadow, Jim Mullins calmly pulled a radio from a hook on his belt. The middle-aged rancher called up his wrangler at Lazy B. "Bob, this is Jim. We have four units up at Wigwam Meadow, four units at Wigwam. We're bringing them in."

Kirstie's heart raced as she listened to the message and the four red cows raised their heads at the disturbance. It looked like two mothers and their spring calves; wary, clumsy creatures with enormous square heads and long, straight backs. Their bellies bulged after a summer's lush feeding, their nervous bellows signaled that they had no intention of being chased and caught.

She saw them break for the nearest trees and

warned Jim that his cattle were about to take cover. The rancher put away his radio. He cupped his hands around his mouth, hollered to Matt, Charlie, and Hadley for help, then rode Monty hard after the cows.

"C'mon, git up!" Kirstie urged Crazy Horse. It would be hard to flush the cows out of the trees again, she knew. So she raced across the clearing, heading around the back of the brushwood at the far side, joining Jim in a scissors movement that would cut the lumbering cattle off before they made it to the dark stand of ponderosas.

"Good, we'll flush 'em out!" the rancher yelled, standing clear of his saddle, racing Monty at a hard gallop.

Realizing what was happening, the cows bunched and turned back toward the clearing. They crashed through undergrowth, stumbling and jostling, bellowing as they went. Now their plan was to bolt back across the meadow, then down the slope toward the creek. But they hadn't banked on Matt and Charlie, who appeared at the edge of the clearing on Cadillac and Rocky, closely followed by Hadley on Moose. Enraged that their escape was blocked, they thundered on.

"Don't get in front!" Jim called. "Keep left, Matt! Keep right, Charlie! Kirstie, you stay behind!"

She got the point and rode alongside Monty, helping to push the cattle through the funnel made by the three riders at the far side of the clearing. Crossing the churned-up meadow, she tucked Crazy Horse in close behind one of the calves, forcing it down the steep hill toward the creek.

"Yee-hah!" Matt took off his hat and raised it above his head as gradually the riders outflanked and tired the fleeing cattle. The four creatures were brought safely down 500 feet of hillside, splashing through water downstream in the direction of Lazy B.

Kirstie grinned at her brother. His face was alive and flushed and there was success in his eyes as they drove the cattle on.

"Steady and slow!" Jim ordered. He saw that the fight had gone out of the tired creatures. It was a long plod home along the creek, watching their woolly white heads sink lower as the morning wore on and the roundup reached its end in a crowded, dusty corral.

\* \* \*

"Great team!" Matt crowed as they rode home to Half Moon Ranch. They'd been out again in the afternoon, rounding up seven more cattle. Now, as the sun sank low behind the mountains, Hadley had stayed on at Lazy B to check brands for Jim Mullins while Charlie, Kirstie, and Matt headed for home.

"We did good," Charlie agreed. He fell into a low, rambling whistle as Rocky, Cadillac, and, last of all, Crazy Horse followed the Meltwater Trail.

"Better than good!" Matt insisted. "We did great!"

Picking up his rider's good mood, Cadillac stepped out smartly over fallen logs, jumping neatly across any gully that came his way.

From behind, Kirstie grinned to herself. Was this the same brother who'd been moping around the house all weekend? Under her breath, she sang the words to the tune Charlie was whistling.

"You know something, Charlie?" Matt went on, his tall figure straight in the saddle, Stetson tipped back on his head. He seemed to forget about Kirstie and Crazy Horse ambling along behind.

"Nope."

"I reckon you got it just about right when you quit school early."

No answer from Charlie, whose whistle, however, picked up speed.

"Like, you knew no way was studying your thing. You looked long and hard at what you were doing and decided to quit. Took a job out here instead. Now you do what you love, day in, day out..." Matt sighed and fell deep into thought.

"I ain't necessarily quit school for good," Charlie reminded him. "Part of taking the job at the ranch is for me to make enough money to get back there if I want."

"...No exams, no sitting in a classroom."

No license to be a vet at the end of it, Kirstie thought. She felt the back of her neck begin to prickle with alarm as Matt went on. That was the deal: Matt studied to be a veterinarian while Sandy paid his way. Their mom wanted to see him take up a good career, and it had been Matt's lifelong ambition to work with animals. The course in Denver seemed to be the ideal solution. But now he was two years into it and evidently changing his mind.

"Take me," he told Charlie. "I ain't the kind of guy you can put behind a desk. I look at Jim Mullins and his life, and I envy him. When did he last sit in an office? And it ain't just me I'm thinking of. There's Mom. You've seen how hard she has to work to keep the place going. Now, if I was there helping out, instead of wasting my time studying—jeez, think how much easier that would be!"

Charlie said nothing. Instead he took up whistling again, this time much more quietly and slowly. Coming up against a clutter of logs that half-blocked a stream, he dismounted to clear the jam.

Quickly, Kirstie jumped off Crazy Horse to help. She seized the end of a log and hauled it free, unsettled by Matt's conversation. She knew that their mother had no idea that this was how he was thinking. "C'mon, Matt, grab the end of this big log!" she called.

"Huh?" Matt frowned as Cadillac backed up away from the stream. His horse didn't like the splash of the foaming white water or the splinter of rotten logs as Charlie hauled another free. Resting on his haunches, he reared up, caught his rider unawares, and tipped him from the saddle. "Hey!" Matt ended up in the dirt with a sore butt and a surprised expression.

"Quick, grab Cadillac!" Charlie hissed at Kirstie. The temperamental gray horse was seizing his chance to lope off home without a rider. His reins flew free about his neck as his long mane whipped from side to side, and he reared again before setting off solo down the track.

Kirstie reached out to grab the reins. Too late. Cadillac twisted and began to run. "Go get him back!" she told Crazy Horse on the spur of the moment, knowing that if anyone could fetch the Thoroughbred back, he could.

For a start, he understood as much as any horse she'd ever known. Inside that ugly-beautiful head of his was a smart brain. He knew that Cadillac was well out of order throwing Matt and loping off. So he set off after him at a strong gallop, overtaking him and then performing one of his spectacular sliding stops. Thirty feet down the trail, in a cloud of brown dust, both horses came to a halt.

Kirstie set off from the stream at a run, followed by Charlie and then Matt. Crazy Horse nudged Cadillac around to face them, stood in his way in case he tried another silly trick, waited until they arrived and took hold of his reins. Within seconds,

Matt had grabbed the horn and hoisted himself back into the saddle. He gathered the reins and slipped his feet into the deep stirrups, shamefaced but back in control.

"Say thanks," Kirstie reminded him as, minutes later, they set off on the final leg of their journey.

"Huh?" Matt had quickly lapsed into his preoccupied daze.

"Say thanks to Crazy Horse," she insisted. "Without him, you'd be walking home!"

"Yeah, yeah!"

No proper thank you; nothing.

"That's brothers for you," Kirstie told Crazy Horse as she brushed him down and gave him his favorite feed of alfalfa hay. "'Thank you' isn't a phrase in their vocabulary!"

Cadillac stood tethered to a nearby post. His head was up and he was looking down his nose at his empty hay net, stamping his feet for attention.

"See ya, Kirstie!" Matt yelled from the yard. He opened his car door, ready to climb in for the drive back to Denver.

She glanced up. "Yeah, see ya!...Good luck on

your exams!" After all, he was under pressure. She excused his lack of gratitude toward Crazy Horse and wished him well.

With one long leg already inside the car, Matt seemed to change his mind. He turned and walked toward her, stopping at the fence. "Hey, you won't, like, say anything to Mom about me quitting school?" he muttered. A deep frown creased his forehead and half-hid his hazel eyes.

Kirstie gave Crazy Horse his last handful of alfalfa and frowned back.

" 'Cause I ain't exactly made up my mind, you understand? Maybe I'll quit. Maybe I'll stay. You know what I mean?"

This time, she nodded.

"OK, good!" He seemed relieved. Reaching out to give Cadillac a gentle rub on his supple cream neck, he jumped down from the fence. Seconds later, the car door slammed, the engine started up, and he was gone.

"Should I? Should I not?" Kirstie asked Crazy Horse and Cadillac. It was one of those problems without a right answer. She'd tried to tease it out as she finished feeding the horses and led them both back to Red Fox Meadow. The sun had gone down, the herd of horses ran restlessly and silently by the far fence. "Should I warn Mom that Matt is thinking of quitting school?" she asked Cadillac.

The beautiful horse looked vacantly at her as she released him from his head collar. He tossed his head, waiting impatiently for Crazy Horse.

"Or should I keep quiet like he asked?" she asked the funny-looking quarter horse.

The tan coat of the stocky gelding looked chocolate-brown in the deep dusk. His long ears flicked and twitched, he lowered his heavy head to nuzzle her hand.

"OK, I know; you don't have the answer, either," she sighed, stroking his soft muzzle, feeling the rough lick of his tongue.

She watched him turn to join his ghostly colored friend.

"Thanks anyway," she whispered, looking up at the new moon, then walking quickly back across the footbridge to the ranch.

**3**

That night, Kirstie found it hard to sleep. She had the window open, as usual, and lay watching the light drapes billow and float in the breeze. Outside, the midnight sky was peppered with sparkling pin-pricks of silver light.

*Should I or shouldn't I warn Mom?* She still sought an answer to the Matt problem long after the house was silent.

*I didn't really promise out loud that I'd keep quiet,* she reminded herself. *When he asked me, I just kinda nodded.* Not like a real promise.

*But he trusts you.* Another voice swooped into her head. Kirstie sat up in bed. Where had that come from?

*So? Mom trusts me, too. She'd be real cut up to learn I was keeping this from her.*

*And what good would it do if you warned her? Say you get up tomorrow, go down, and announce that Matt wants to quit school. What then?* The voice cut across her conviction that Sandy should know what her son was planning. *And maybe he doesn't really want to quit. What if he gets back to Denver and decides he loves his college course, after all? You know what he's like. You can never tell with Matt whether he means what he says.*

Unsettled, Kirstie got out of bed and drifted toward the window. She leaned her elbows on the sill and gazed out across the yard. *I just figure that Mom would rather know,* she countered. *Maybe then she could call Matt and talk it through.*

*Uh-oh.* The voice warned against it. Strangely, it had begun to sound like Lisa, and Kirstie kept getting flashes of her friend's intense green eyes, of her pale face surrounded by dark red curls. *Can you think of anything more guaranteed to make him quit? You know he always does the exact opposite of what folks want him to do!*

Sighing at this, she stared up at the stars. *Help!* No response. They sparkled on in the blue velvet sky.

Kirstie turned to go back to bed. But out of the corner of her eye, she caught a movement down below. In the shadow of the great mountains, on the far side of the creek. She peered through the darkness. She couldn't see exactly what was happening, but she could hear something... Horses! Hooves drumming up and down the meadow, a restless turning and bunching together, a touch of fear in the air.

Was it a mountain lion? A bear? It would be rare but not unheard of for either to creep down from Eagle's Peak to stalk the valley herd. Yet the horses were behaving strangely; she could still hear their hooves, and now and then, a high whinny from one to another. Danger!

Horses were flight animals. In the wild, instinct told them to bunch together and run from predators like lions or coyotes. And that's what the horses in the remuda seemed to be trying to do. Penned in by strong fences, they thundered around the meadow in growing panic.

*Hmm.* Kirstie went back to the window and peered out. It was probably nothing. Horses spooked easily, especially at night. And whatever it was out there was most likely just poking around the garbage cans at the back of the cookhouse. Still, she'd better go check. Seeing that it was a frosty night, she slipped a fleece jacket over her pajamas, stepped into her sneakers, and went quietly downstairs.

The cold air hit her the second she stepped out onto the porch. Blowing down off Eagle's Peak, it cut through the thick jacket and made her gasp. Clutching the collar around her chin, she ventured out into the yard.

Still the horses charged inside their confined space. The sound of their hooves was louder, their whinnies carried on the wind. It seemed they were bunched together at the near end of the meadow, taking refuge not from some menace close to the ranch house but from a danger at the far side, where the fence came up against a sudden cliff of bare granite— a natural barrier between Half Moon Ranch and a stretch of national forest beyond.

What could it be? Now that she was down here, Kirstie found she couldn't so easily dismiss the disturbance. She glanced back at the house. Her mom's bedroom window was dark. Sandy was sleeping through the noise. So was Charlie, whose bunkhouse light was off. She'd better investigate, then, if necessary, wake the others.

Trying to look more confident than she felt, she ran across the footbridge, her footsteps silent, her skin tingling with cold. She could make out Lucky's pale mane and tail in the bunch of horses clustered by the gate, saw him pick up her presence, detach himself from the herd, and lope alongside the fence to greet her. The other horses jostled closer together, but as her eyes grew used to the dark, she could pick out Yukon's distinctive brown and white coat and Johnny Mohawk's jet-black shape rising like a shadow onto his hind legs, eyes gleaming, tail lashing from side to side.

"OK, Lucky, what is it?" Kirstie reached the white fence and mounted the bottom rung. She leaned out to pat the palomino's neck, felt it was cold and clammy to the touch. "Wow, something sure spooked you!" she murmured.

There was a sudden crack, like wood splintering. It sent the whole herd into a frenzy of rearing and stamping. Lucky flinched, his head high, eyes staring across the meadow. Another crack from the far end of the field sent the bunched horses galloping, leaving Lucky quivering at Kirstie's side.

The thing to do, if she wanted to get close enough to discover what the heck was going on, was to slip onto Lucky and ride bareback to join the herd. Before she had time to consider the danger, she'd climbed the fence. Lucky stood still just long enough for her to jump on, then he was away, galloping like crazy to catch up with the rest.

Kirstie leaned forward, arms around her horse's neck, body flat against him as his powerful stride took her across the rough grass. She had to cling on and concentrate hard to keep her balance, rolling with his gait, judging the speed by the wind in her hair. Then, as soon as he joined the herd, he slowed and gave her time to look up. Surrounded by horses, she was hidden in their midst as she tried to make out what was happening in the deep shadow of the cliff.

It seemed that there were more horses over

there—possibly as many as four or five. Nothing odd in that, maybe. But when one came out of the shadow and she spotted a rider on its back, she froze. *Who on earth? What on earth?*

Without seeing Kirstie, the man reined his horse harshly, wheeled him around and vanished back into the shadow. There was another sharp sound of wood breaking, a muffled shout, before Lucky and the herd veered away.

They were crashing through the fence! There must be more than one rider. They were stealing Half Moon horses! This was the only explanation. Kirstie clung to Lucky and raced him back the length of the meadow, using her legs to steer him close to the gate and slow him so that she could jump off and raise the alarm. Shocked and trembling, she vaulted the fence and ran for the bunkhouse, rattling on Charlie's door, then racing on to warn her mom.

"Mom, quick! Call the cops! There are horse rustlers out in Red Fox Meadow! C'mon, get up, please!" She took the stairs two at a time, flung open Sandy's door, switched on the light. Her mom raised her head and groaned.

"Wake up!" Then she was out on the landing and down the stairs, heading back to the bunkhouse to find Charlie staggering out, sleepy and disheveled. "Come quick!" she pleaded. "Bring a shotgun. We've got rustlers...stealing the horses...quick, or we'll be too late!"

And now they all three gathered their wits and ran. Sandy Scott had brought a flashlight, which she turned on, swinging the beam across the field. The herd stampeded, coats glistening with sweat in the moonlight, taking a crazy course around the meadow, churning up the ground. They reared and cried out, thudded down, whirled and spun in a frenzy of fear.

"Over there!" Charlie cried. The flashlight beam had picked out the activity at the far end of the meadow. The young wrangler ran toward the cliff, rifle in hand.

Three figures on horseback saw the light, heard Charlie's voice. They circled the two horses they'd cut out from the herd and drove them toward the gap in the fence, forcing them out of the field before their pursuers on foot could stop them.

Three men! Kirstie strained to take in the details.

Stetsons and thick jackets with collars turned up. Leather chaps flapping against their saddles, one with a fancy plaited bridle in white and red. The flashlight picked it out; it was unusual, something to fix in her mind. But the men's faces were hidden under the brims of their hats, and their heads were down as they drove the chosen horses out of the field.

"They're turning them toward the creek!" Sandy gasped, then lost the rustlers as they rode out of range of her flashlight. She stopped running and looked wildly around. "We'll never move fast enough without horses."

"Let's try cutting them off!" Charlie realized that the thieves were heading the two stolen horses through the narrow gap between the granite cliff and Five Mile Creek, moving them upstream, away from the ranch. From the sound of their shouted commands and counter-commands, they knew that the first rider had reached the water and plunged in. The others stayed behind the Half Moon Ranch horses, yelling and urging them on into the stream.

Kirstie groaned. "Too late!" She'd lost too much time running to raise the alarm. She should have stopped and tried to tackle the rustlers by herself.

Charlie saw that she was right. He, Sandy, and Kirstie stood helpless in the meadow with horses weaving to the left and right. Raising his gun, he took aim at the backs of the escaping rustlers. "Do you want me to shoot?"

In the dark? At moving targets? With horses rearing and going crazy in between? Kirstie put her hands to her face.

There was a long pause as the stolen horses splashed into the stream and the now-invisible thieves drove them on.

"No," Sandy sighed. "Too dangerous. Let's face it, we already lost them."

"I'm gonna check which horses they took!" Charlie did the first thing that came to mind while Sandy ran to the ranch to call the police.

Kirstie felt sick with a sense of failure. She stood by the broken fence, staring emptily into the darkness.

"You fill in the gap in the fence!" Charlie yelled. "Prop posts against the broken section. Get a move on, Kirstie, before the rest of the horses get it into their heads to escape!"

She broke out of her daze and clicked into action,

dragging broken sections of fence into position, ignoring the panicky hooves still drumming up and down the field. The rustlers had chosen to crash through at the point farthest from the ranch, hoping, no doubt, to do their work and be gone before anyone heard them. It had been their bad luck that Kirstie had lain awake, come to the window, and discovered what they were up to.

*Not that I was any use!* She blamed herself for not using her head. *I didn't even get a decent description to give to the sheriff!* Angrily, she jammed planks back into position as best she could.

"That's fine." Sandy Scott came back out and told Kirstie that the makeshift repair should hold until morning. "I had to wake Larry Francini out of bed," she reported. "He says he'll be out this way to talk to us some time tomorrow."

Stepping back from the fence, Kirstie grunted. "By that time, they'll be miles away. Why can't he come now?"

"With a posse of deputies?" Sandy sighed. "Get real, Kirstie. This is two plain old quarter horses we're talking about here, remember. You don't get a squad of cars with blue flashing lights driving twenty-five miles out from San Luis in the middle of the night for a couple of ranch horses."

They turned as Charlie finished checking out the herd and came striding toward them.

"Well?" Sandy asked, her voice strained. "Which ones did they take?"

But before he could answer, Kirstie grabbed her mom's arm and pointed. She'd seen something moving, high up the valley, across a pale patch of ground on the hillside. From the shape of the rocks on the horizon, she could pick out Miners' Ridge, and directly below that, the pale patch, which must be the flat ledge of Hummingbird Rock. "I reckon that's them!" she gasped.

Yes, there were figures on horseback, tiny from this distance, but silhouetted against the rock, the stars and moonlight strong enough to pick them out. And there were two horses not being ridden; the two stolen from the meadow. One was dark and difficult to identify, but the other was much lighter—a big, pale horse struggling and pulling against the rope tied tight around his neck. A pure gray horse.

"Cadillac!" Kirstie whispered.

"Right," Charlie muttered.

The most valuable horse in the remuda. Matt's beautiful pedigree.

"And who else?" Sandy asked.

Kirstie stared up the hillside at the dark horse fighting his captors at the end of a short, cruel rope. The horse strained and twisted, raised himself onto his hind legs, and sent an eerie, angry cry echoing down the valley. He was smaller and heavier than the gray Thoroughbred and still straining against the rope as the rustlers forced him along the length of Hummingbird Rock.

"Crazy Horse," Charlie reported after a long silence. "That's who they took. Matt's two horses, Cadillac and Crazy Horse."

**4**

"Why would anyone in their right mind steal Crazy Horse?" Lisa demanded.

She stood with Kirstie outside the main school entrance as kids streamed in for the start of morning classes. Yellow buses dropped them off in droves, and they trekked across a yard whitened by a light covering of overnight snow. Several jostled by with curious glances, wondering why the two girls stood on the step deep in conversation.

"Please, Lisa, don't start on that again!" Kirstie's shoulders dropped, her eyes prickled from lack of sleep. She'd ridden in on the bus hoping for sympathy from the person she considered to be her best friend. Yet all Lisa could do was point out one more time how lacking poor Crazy Horse was in the equine beauty stakes.

"No, I'm serious!" Lisa opened her eyes wide and spread both hands palms upward. "Why Crazy Horse?"

Kirstie turned to follow the latest arrivals into school. "Maybe they have a problem judging what makes a good horse," she said sarcastically. "You don't have to be an expert on how a horse should look to steal one!"

"No!" Lisa ran up the steps after her. "I really mean it, Kirstie. I'm being logical here. Crazy Horse doesn't have any kind of pedigree, does he?"

Slowly, Kirstie faced her. "Oh, yeah. His mother was a purebred Arab, his sire was Independence Day, a Kentucky Thoroughbred from one of the best studs in the country! Didn't I tell you?"

Ignoring her scathing remark, Lisa rushed on. "So, no pedigree. Nothing special to pick him out from any other horse in the remuda?"

"You got it." Giving up any hope of a sympathetic response, Kirstie headed down the corridor to her classroom.

"But you haven't!" Lisa was still close on her heels. "Got my point, that is. Which is: it could've been Yukon or Jitterbug. But it wasn't. It was Crazy Horse."

"Wrong place, wrong time, I guess." Poor Crazy Horse just happened to be the nearest victim. The rope had snaked out across the meadow and his had been the head that the noose had fallen over.

"But isn't it too much of a coincidence? Doesn't Crazy Horse stick by Cadillac, come hell or high water?" Lisa slipped in through the classroom doorway and put her arm across it to block Kirstie's way. "They're the same as Lucky and Rodeo Rocky; you can't pry them apart. So what if the real plan was just to steal Cadillac? Wouldn't that make more sense?"

"Maybe." Kirstie was forced to think the theory through. "Cadillac's worth twice as much money as any other horse we have. But when the rustlers roped him and began to drag him out of the field, you reckon Crazy Horse must have objected?"

Lisa nodded. "He'd see he was losing his best friend. It's the middle of the night and these strange guys break in and take Cadillac prisoner. He'd go crazy, wouldn't he?"

Kirstie nodded. "He'd put up a big fight to stay with Cadillac, that's for sure."

"So the only way the rustlers would make it was if they took Crazy Horse along, too." Lisa saw that her argument had finally sunk in. "He played the hero and gave up his own freedom for Cadillac!"

"Right." Kirstie closed her eyes and thought hard. A scary question shaped itself out of the turmoil of the previous night's events. "But if the rustlers don't really want Crazy Horse, and they only used him to get Cadillac out of the meadow…" she paused to look Lisa straight in the eye, "…then what's gonna happen to the poor guy now?"

"Kirstie, I'm real sorry." Lisa sought Kirstie out during lunch break. She found her outside in the empty yard, sitting on a low wall and huddled inside her fleece jacket.

"Yeah, I know." A loud sigh escaped from deep in her chest. Kirstie had been hoping that her gloomy mood would ease during the morning. But it hadn't. If anything, it had gotten worse. Here she was in school, not hearing a word anyone said to her. In English her teacher had called her out for daydreaming, and in math, she'd stumbled over an easy question.

"No, you don't." Lisa shivered, then sat quietly beside her. Together, they stared down San Luis's long main street. "I don't mean I'm sorry about Cadillac and Crazy Horse..."

Kirstie bit her lip and narrowed her eyes. She spotted the sheriff's car pulling away from his office and cruising toward the school.

"...But sure I am." Lisa pulled herself up short. "I reckon it's a shame about the robbery."

Kirstie turned a troubled gaze toward her friend. "Where are they now?" she pleaded. "Are they in a truck being driven to some sale barn somewhere? Are they holed up in some nasty, dark barn? Where?"

Lisa shook her head, struggling to say what she felt. "Listen, I feel bad, I want to tell you...the other day, I was way out of line."

Giving an empty smile, Kirstie sighed again. "You gave Crazy Horse a pretty hard time," she admitted.

"I know. And that's why I'm sorry. If I'd known

he was gonna be stolen, I'd never have been so rough on him. And now he's gone, and it feels like it's my fault."

"No way." Kirstie softened. "But thanks anyway."

As the sheriff's car drew near and eased into the curb, Lisa nodded. "So we're OK, you and me?"

Kirstie nodded back. Sheriff Francini had gotten out of the car, was zipping up his jacket and heading toward her. "Hey, Lisa," she murmured before her friend could slip away. "Don't feel bad."

"No?" Lisa hesitated. "How come?"

For the first time since the incident, Kirstie smiled. "You were right. Crazy Horse doesn't score high marks in the looks department. I'm not saying he's ugly, mind; just unusual. And you know something? He kinda makes up for it."

"Great personality," Lisa confirmed.

"Smart," Kirstie added. "Real clever."

"A kidder."

"Yeah, a joker," Kirstie agreed. "And I guess I have to admit, just a *little* bit nutty."

Sheriff Larry Francini looked and sounded more like the man who ran the local pizza restaurant than the upholder of law and order in San Luis County, Colorado. He was short—stocky if you were kind, fat if you were honest—and had a fringe of dark hair below a shiny bald head. He wore a dark mustache and a permanent, easygoing smile.

"Don't be too hard on yourself," he told Kirstie after she'd tried to describe the three horse thieves from the night before. "Your mom tells me it was pretty dark out there. Ain't no surprise to me that you don't remember too much about them."

"You seen my mom?" Kirstie sat in the principal's office with the sheriff. She'd been excused from the first class of the afternoon to talk to him.

"Sure. I was out there this morning. Helped Charlie and her fix the fence. According to her, it was you who raised the alarm."

"Yes, but I wish I'd concentrated more on how they looked. All I know is there were three of them, wearing Stetsons, collars up."

"How about their horses?"

"One was a sorrel, two were paints." Kirstie remembered this much, at least. "Oh, and one was wearing a fancy bridle; one of those plaited kinds, red and white leather, I guess. It looked new to me."

"Hmm." The sheriff made a mental note. "Maybe I could check that with the local saddlery store, see if an item like that has been sold lately."

Kirstie nodded quickly. It was the only detail so far that might provide a lead. "What else are you gonna do?" she urged.

"Well, now, first I file my report…"

"No, I mean, where are you gonna start looking for Cadillac and Crazy Horse?"

Larry Francini stood and picked up his white felt hat from the principal's desk. "It ain't that easy. For a start, we don't have too many clues to go on."

Kirstie broke in. "They were headed up by Hummingbird Rock. We saw them there, heading for Miners' Ridge. Isn't that a start?"

Francini went on steadily. "Second, I'm a little short of men right now. My deputy is on vacation, and I have a whole stack of traffic violations piling up on my desk, plus a break-in at the gas station last Friday night…"

This was bad news for Kirstie. "You mean, you won't be going after the rustlers?"

Hat on head, the sheriff shrugged. "I mean to keep my eyes and ears open," he promised on his way out of the door. "Once I've filed the report, I reckon that's about the best I can do."

"That's the real world." Later that afternoon, Sandy Scott sat Kirstie down at the kitchen table. "You can't expect all the cops in Colorado to drop everything and go out onto Miners' Ridge looking for Cadillac and Crazy Horse!"

"I don't want all the cops in the whole state, just a couple!" Frustrated and angry, Kirstie flopped into a chair and fought back the tears. "When did the sheriff's office in San Luis last arrest a criminal? That's what I want to know!"

Sandy frowned and glanced at Lisa, who had ridden out with Kirstie to Half Moon Ranch on the school bus. Kirstie's mother looked pale and tired, resigned to what had happened.

"I agree." Lisa defended her friend. "If they were my horses, I'd want Sheriff Francini to visit Jim Mullins at the Lazy B for a start. That's the next ranch to here, so there's a good chance the rustlers had to pass through Horseshoe Valley around about dawn."

"Maybe." Sandy Scott nodded. "And I'm sure the sheriff will do that when he finds the time."

"Yeah!" Kirstie had paid attention to Lisa's theory. "Once you come down the far side of Miners' Ridge, the dirt track running along Horseshoe Creek is the only road for miles. That's where the rustlers must have parked their truck!"

"Maybe!" her mom repeated, more loudly this time, and with a note of warning not to rush ahead without thinking.

But Kirstie jumped up from the table. "Is Hadley still over there?" she demanded. "Why don't we give him a call and ask him what he saw?"

"Cool it." Running a hand through her hair, Sandy motioned into the living room for Charlie to begin loading bales of hay onto the pickup truck to drive out to Red Fox Meadow. The young wrangler got off the phone, stepped outside, and got to work. "I already thought of Hadley and called the Lazy B," Sandy went on. "He says they slept through the night. No one at the ranch saw anything suspicious."

The news seemed to put to rest the only good theory the girls had had so far. "Back to square one," Lisa muttered.

"Farther back than that," Kirstie said bleakly,

slumping down at the table once more. "Square one minus one!"

"And you know what?" Sandy hovered by the living-room door. She picked up a cup of coffee which she'd allowed to go cold, took a sip, then threw out the dregs. "There's one phone call I didn't make, and that was to Denver to tell Matt what happened."

Kirstie listed the reasons why not. She'd sprung into life at the mention of her brother's name, crossed the room, and told her mom not to pick up the phone.

"Number one, he's in an exam room right this minute, so no one gets to speak to him. Two, you can't just leave a message; you have to give him the bad news person to person. Three, he has more tests later this week. If you tell him about Crazy Horse and Cadillac now, he'll want to skip his exams and come right home!"

What she still didn't tell Sandy was that Matt was already on the brink of quitting his course. The news about his beloved horses would definitely be the final straw.

"I know!" Her mom began to pace up and down

the hallway. "Why do you think I've been putting it off?"

"You have to tell him sooner or later," Lisa pointed out quietly. She glanced apologetically at Kirstie. "If it was me, I guess I'd really want to know."

"But we should wait!" To Kirstie, it seemed vital.

"For what?" Lisa held steadily to her opinion. She raised her eyebrows. "For Sheriff Francini to make an arrest?"

"No. For...for Matt to finish his exams," Kirstie faltered.

"And?" Sandy Scott was caught between a rock and a hard place. She genuinely wanted to know what else Kirstie had in mind.

The idea, when it came, was the obvious one that they should all have thought of much sooner.

"For a few of us to ride out onto Hummingbird Rock," Kirstie suggested. "That was the last place we saw the horses. Surely, someone should go take a look!"

Because it could do no harm, Sandy agreed to let Charlie ride out to the rock with Kirstie and Lisa.

"After he's finished feeding the horses in the remuda," she insisted. "That will still give you a few hours of daylight: enough time to find out if the rustlers left any clues."

"And you promise not to call Matt while we're gone?" Filled with sudden energy, Kirstie quickly lent Lisa some jeans and a sweatshirt, and the girls changed out of their school clothes, ready to saddle Lucky, Jitterbug, and Rodeo Rocky.

"I promise," Sandy agreed with a troubled frown. "If you promise me not to do anything crazy."

"Me?" Kirstie joked, pulling on her boots, reaching for her cap.

"Yes, you." Sandy followed them to the door. "Remember, the trail gets steep and narrow up there. It's below freezing, so there'll be ice on the ground. You just take it easy."

Exchanging promises, tightening cinch buckles, checking stirrups, they tacked up, ready to ride.

Sandy held Lucky's reins as Kirstie sprang into the saddle.

"We'll be back before dark, no problem," Kirstie assured her. It felt good to be doing something positive at last. "And Mom, there's bound to be clues: footprints, a trail of some kind."

"You hope!" Her mother smiled and let go of the reins.

"I know!" Kirstie said as she pointed Lucky out of the corral and over the footbridge. "It'll all slide into place once we're up on the rock. I get this weird feeling we're gonna find out exactly what happened to those two horses out there on Hummingbird Rock!"

**5**

Snow weighed down the branches of the lodge-pole pines. It slipped and thudded gently to the ground as Kirstie, Lisa, and Charlie guided their horses up the mountain. Small flakes floated in the air, settling and melting on their faces. Their gazes were fixed on the narrow trail. Far ahead, at 13,000 feet, the jagged outline of Eagle's Peak appeared, then disappeared behind a blanket of heavy gray clouds.

"How much snow has fallen since last night?" Lisa asked Charlie, her voice uneasy.

"Not much. Couple of inches." He brushed against a branch. A heavy fall of frozen snow slid onto his yellow waterproof slicker, then hit the ground.

"But enough to hide hoofprints," Lisa pointed out. She was looking in vain for the trail left by the rustlers the night before.

Up ahead on Lucky, Kirstie ignored them. Though the air was freezing, she felt hot and uncomfortable under her own plastic slicker, which Sandy had made her wear. It was probably anxiety that had raised her body temperature, she realized, because if she was honest with herself, the confidence she'd expressed before they set out had soon vanished, and now she shared Lisa's doubts about picking up clues.

"Yeah, you can forget hoofprints," Charlie agreed, examining the smooth, white covering of snow on the trail. They were approaching the level ledge of Hummingbird Rock in single file— Kirstie, then Lisa, then Charlie. "Look for other signs," he warned.

"Like what?" Kirstie reached the ledge and stopped. From here, she had a clear view of the sweep of hills and valleys that surrounded their ranch.

"Like this broken branch." Charlie pointed out the damage to a nearby pine. "That happened since we rode this way to Lazy B."

Kirstie nodded eagerly. "I remember, this was the place where Crazy Horse put up a fight. I could see him kicking and fighting as they dragged him along the ledge. Hey, and here's a flattened bush!"

Glad to see the obvious signs, she slipped from the saddle to examine the ground.

"Anything?" Lisa leaned sideways out of Jitterbug's saddle. The sorrel mare stood quite still, listening intently to the unfamiliar, muffled sounds around.

"Nope. The ground's frozen solid beneath the snow. There's a hoofprint or two, but nothing much to go on...Hey, look at this!" Stooping under the bush, Kirstie reached until her fingertips made contact with a coil of rope which she'd spotted. She brushed off the snow, then held it up for the others to see.

"The guys last night must have dropped it,"

Charlie said, taking it from her. "Leastways, it sure don't belong to Half Moon Ranch."

The rope was new and expensive looking, the natural fibers intertwined with distinctive threads of red and white. Kirstie realized that it matched the fancy bridle on one of the rustlers' horses.

"We can take it to Sheriff Francini as evidence," Lisa suggested.

Rodeo Rocky shifted and snorted. Like Jitterbug, he was on edge, swishing his black tail and flicking his ears. "OK, tie the rope to your saddle," Charlie ordered Kirstie. "Let's get the horses moving, see what we can spot from the ridge."

So Kirstie remounted, and they moved on, from Hummingbird Rock along Meltwater Trail to Miners' Ridge, looking all the time for more evidence of the rustlers' track. At the ridge, they stopped again.

"Decision time," Charlie insisted. "Do we follow the trail to Lazy B, or do we turn back and head for home?"

Kirstie glanced back the way they'd come, then down the steep, wooded slopes of Jim Mullins's property. At the bottom of the valley, there were glimpses of the winding course of Horseshoe Creek running silver between dark rocks where the snow had melted. Down there, beside the stream, was the dirt road that led to Lazy B; possibly the route the thieves had taken during their escape with Cadillac and Crazy Horse. "Let's find out what Jim knows," she decided.

So they went gingerly on, taking their time on the icy surface, leaning back in the saddle as the horses picked their way. Even so, Jitterbug slipped and skidded into Lucky, who stood fast to save horse and rider from losing control on the steep descent.

"Close!" Lisa breathed as she pulled herself upright in the saddle, looking back at the scuffed, dirty snow where her horse had lost her footing.

"We're almost at the road," Charlie reassured them. This time, he and Rocky led the way until they reached the creek at the spot where they'd brought the four cows down from Wigwam Meadow the day before.

Without speaking, head down and collar up against the light, whirling snowflakes, Kirstie joined him and reined Lucky to the right, pressing on along the level road toward the cattle ranch.

But before she'd covered many feet, she heard Lisa's voice calling from behind.

"Hey, what's this bridge?"

Kirstie swung around to look over her shoulder. "What bridge?"

"Across the creek." Lisa faced the other way, pointing to some rough wooden planks that spanned the banks. "I never knew this was here! Where does it lead to?"

"It's new, I guess." Never having noticed it herself, Kirstie turned to Charlie for an answer.

The wrangler nodded. "Wes Logan's men put it up a couple of weeks back. That's Ponderosa Pines land on the far bank. Logan wanted a bridge to bring cattle across and truck them out through Jim Mullins's territory to join up with the San Luis highway. It's a kind of shortcut for him."

Kirstie frowned. She knew, as a rule, how jealously the ranchers guarded the boundaries of their own land. "How come Jim said it was OK?"

Charlie shrugged. "I reckon Logan had to pay for the privilege. And Jim would charge him plenty."

"Never mind that now," Lisa broke in. "The bridge is there, and it means there's a chance that the horse thieves didn't head down past Jim's ranch house after all…"

"…Which is why Hadley says they all slept through the night without any disturbances!" Kirstie said.

"…Because they crossed the creek and took a way out to the road through Wes Logan's place!" Lisa made her theory sound convincing. She was all for reining the horses to the left and taking up the new trail.

"Through Ponderosa Pines?" Kirstie trotted Lucky alongside Jitterbug. A suspicion began to gnaw away at her. "Or *to* it? Listen, what if the rustlers came this way, over the bridge, up onto the ridge, and down onto our land to steal Cadillac?"

"From Ponderosa Pines?" Charlie sounded uncomfortable. "That means Wes Logan was in on it. Is that what you're saying?"

Kirstie nodded hard. "And I'll tell you why. A couple of days back, Mr. Logan called my mom. He wanted to buy Cadillac for his wife to ride."

"She said no?" Lisa picked it up fast. "So he gets mad. He decides he wants the horse anyway, sends his men out in the middle of the night…"

"No way!" Charlie wouldn't listen to it. "Too risky. The guy would have to be crazy!"

Kirstie and Lisa sat side by side. "So?"

"So, Wes Logan is a straight-down-the-line, regular guy. He has a whole stack of horses, including a real beautiful white mare, San Luis Dawn, and enough dough to buy the whole remuda at Half Moon Ranch. Why would he back a crazy plan like that?"

The girls stared back at him with determined faces. They didn't know the answers. They just had a gut feeling.

"Besides," Charlie went on, "he wouldn't make it so obvious. Why would he call your mom and bring up the fact that he badly wanted this horse?"

Lisa and Kirstie didn't shift.

"It's just too darn...obvious!" the wrangler insisted. He rode Rocky up and down the track, thinking, reluctant to believe it.

"You got a better idea?" Kirstie said at last.


Ponderosa Pines spread out before them. The ranch house was huge. It was surrounded by lawns, a tennis court, an open-air pool. The stables stood back from the house across an immaculate yard where several pickups and one big horse box were parked in a neat row.

"Wow!" Lisa took in the whole spread. "How much did this cost?"

"Millions," Charlie replied. "Wes Logan built the pool before he moved in. He put in walkers and a round pen for the horses. The money he spent was the talk of San Luis County."

"And we're gonna ride in there with: 'Say, Mr. Logan, did you by any chance steal our horses?'" Even Lisa's nerve began to fail.

"Like, yeah," Charlie grumbled through gritted teeth as they walked Rocky, Jitterbug, and Lucky toward the house.

"No, stupid!" Kirstie led the way. "We're gonna ask him if they saw anything suspicious around here last night. We can watch how he reacts. If he looks guilty, we know we're onto something."

"Great," Charlie mumbled. "Smart thinking, Kirstie!"

She turned her wide gray gaze on him, challenging him not to back out. "You ask, we'll stay in the background."

"*Me?*" The young wrangler was still arguing when

a tall figure dressed in jeans and a light tan suede jacket came out of the house onto the porch. He waited there for the three riders to approach.

"Is that him?" Lisa hissed.

"Yep." Kirstie had seen the rich rancher only once before, at a rodeo event in town. But she immediately recognized the thickset, broad-shouldered man with his light brown, wavy hair and clean-shaven, square features. Despite his good looks, he had the kind of face that didn't seem attractive. It never gave anything away—was too set, expressionless, guarded.

"Looks like you had a tough ride." He noted their dripping slickers, the soaked coats of their three horses. "Where did you come from?"

"Half Moon Ranch." Charlie dismounted and introduced himself.

Kirstie studied the man's face. No reaction. Or maybe just a flicker of his eyelids, a glance up at her and Lisa as he shook Charlie's hand.

"We're looking for a couple of our horses," Charlie explained, deliberately laid-back. He took off his sodden leather gloves and tipped the brim of his hat back.

"You lost them?" Keeping to the shelter of the porch, Wes Logan folded his arms.

"Stolen," Charlie said. "Last night, around midnight."

The rancher sniffed. "That's tough. You sure about that?"

"We saw the rustlers," Kirstie told him. She tried to read his reaction, saw him drop his gaze then look sideways toward the stables, where a man was standing in a doorway. "They headed up onto Hummingbird Rock."

"Which is why we're asking you if you spotted anything not right," Charlie went on. He was tensing up, sounding less casual than before. "They could've ridden over the ridge and down in this direction."

Wes Logan shrugged. He seemed perfectly relaxed. "Not a thing. Sorry."

Kirstie glanced at Lisa and frowned.

"No one rode by?"

"I told you, no. What did you lose, a couple of quarter horses?" The rancher's manner suggested it could be no big deal.

"A quarter horse and a Thoroughbred. Good-looking horse, pure gray. The best we had."

74

*Don't pretend you don't know who we're talking about!*
Kirstie said to herself. She saw the moment as a
test for Logan.

"I know him." The rancher nodded briefly. If
anything, his face went blanker than ever. "Nice
horse. Put in an offer for him myself."

"You don't say." It was Charlie's turn to put on
a show.

"Yep. Reckoned he'd be a good match for a
horse of mine. You wanna see?" Without waiting
for an answer, and with an unexpected burst of
hospitality, Wes Logan invited them all across the
yard to the stables. "San Luis Dawn is her name."

"I heard of her," Charlie said. Behind Logan's
back, he shrugged at Lisa and Kirstie, then
gestured for them to dismount and follow.

"What's he up to?" Lisa whispered as she tethered
Jitterbug to a post in the corral.

"I don't know, but I don't trust him," Kirstie
breathed. She took off her slicker and slung it
across Lucky's saddle to save it from getting wet.
Then the two girls ran after the men.

Inside the spacious, airy stables, the rancher was
walking Charlie down a central aisle, pointing out

the good points of this horse, then that. There were two men at work filling hay nets and raking out stalls. They took no notice of the visitors, keeping their backs turned and heads down. Finally, at the far end of the aisle, Wes Logan stopped and stood to one side.

"San Luis Dawn," he said, his voice altering for the first time to include a note of pride.

They were looking into a stall containing a tall, elegant creature the color of cream on top of milk. Her white mane was long and silky, her dark eyes fringed with gray, her nose long and straight, her muzzle soft. She had neat ears pricked forward and a long supple neck.

"Cadillac's double!" Lisa whispered.

"Do you like her?" There was a satisfied smile on the rancher's face as he studied their reactions.

The horse inside the stall raised her head and whinnied. She stamped on the floor with a well-polished hoof and tossed her mane, inviting them to admire her.

"Fabulous!" Kirstie murmured. A horse this beautiful struck at her heart. "Out of this world. Amazing!"

**6**

"I'm c-c-cold!" Lisa complained. "My feet are freezing, I can't feel my fingers, and my face is a solid block of ice!"

Kirstie allowed Lucky to plod ahead, up the slopes of Lazy B land toward Miners' Ridge. Light was fading and snow clouds rolling in. She reckoned they had half an hour of daylight to make it back to Half Moon Ranch.

"Sure was a waste of time back there at Ponderosa Pines," Charlie admitted. "Aside from being given the chance to take a look at the mind-blowing gray mare, of course."

The coil of fancy rope hanging around Kirstie's saddle horn attracted her attention as the others grumbled on. Finding it had been their last lucky break in their quest to trace the horse thieves. After that, the clues had dried up, and even she was questioning her own hunch that Wes Logan had somehow been involved.

"I can sure see why Mr. Logan wanted to buy Cadillac," Charlie went on. "He and San Luis Dawn would look mighty fine."

"Oh, I'm c-c-co-old!" Lisa groaned. She hunched inside her slicker, letting Jitterbug pick her own way up the mountain. "Next time you mix me up in some crazy notion of tracking down a bunch of horse thieves, Kirstie Scott, I just gotta tell myself, 'warm fires, hot chocolate, TV'! 'Cause no way do I want to go through this again. I'd rather stay home like any normal person!"

Kirstie gave a faint smile but no reply. She'd reached the ridge and turned to wait for the other two riders trailing along behind.

"How come you're not telling me to cowboy-up?" Lisa challenged. It was Kirstie's usual way of joking Lisa out of a tough situation. They could be starving hungry out on a trail and the rain could come down in buckets. They would be drenched to the skin, lost miles from anywhere, and Kirstie would drop in the old Half Moon Ranch motto: "C'mon, Lisa, cowboy-up!"

"Hmm? Oh, I guess I'm thinking about Wes Logan's plans for San Luis Dawn," she answered quietly. Charlie and Rodeo Rocky had joined them on the ridge, and this time, she let the wrangler's horse lead the way down onto Meltwater Trail.

"You mean shipping her out to California for the winter?" Lisa recalled the rich rancher's phone conversation about the white horse.

His cell phone had interrupted them as they admired his pride and joy, and he'd answered it to confirm arrangements with his wife, Nancy, for San Luis Dawn to spend the winter in the warmer climate of the West Coast. There'd been talk of two drivers being used to drive the horse box the long distance, mention of times and dates, of a ranch called Bluebird Hill outside San Francisco, and the expected day when "they" would arrive.

The word "they" had bothered Kirstie. "They

should be with you late Sunday," Wes Logan had told his wife down the long-distance line.

Who were "they"? Did it mean he was planning to send more than one horse in the truck? If so, who? One of the other horses in the luxurious stables at Ponderosa Pines? Or did "they" refer to the men who would be driving the truck; presumably two of the silent workers fixing up hay nets and checking water feeders as Kirstie and the others stood admiring the Thoroughbred gray horse?

"Just think what that's gonna cost him!" Lisa went on, regardless of Kirstie's silence. "A horse box like that is worth more than my mom's entire house and diner!"

"A man with that kind of money doesn't care," Charlie cut in, a touch of envy in his voice. "I guess he can do most anything he wants."

Kirstie frowned as Lucky negotiated a slippery section of rock ahead. "Would that include stealing a horse he can't buy legally, by any chance?" she wondered out loud.

"Kirstie!" Lisa sighed. "You need evidence. You need something solid to go on. And what did we find? Zero, zilch, nothing!"

Charlie nodded once, then made Rocky put on speed along a flatter stretch of trail.

"Let it drop," came the advice from Lisa.

The horses broke into a trot, eager to be back.

"I can't!" Kirstie muttered under her breath, her earlier doubts giving way to fresh certainty. *Sure, Logan was smooth and friendly. Sure, he never gave us a clue that he was mixed up in stealing Cadillac and Crazy Horse. But…there was something about him that was not quite right.* The low log cabins of Half Moon Ranch came into view, their red roofs covered in snow. *He knows more than he's saying,* she decided, as Lucky lengthened his stride and loped for home. *And I aim to find out what it is!*

"Matt knows!" Sandy Scott came onto the porch to greet a chilled and dejected Lisa and Kirstie. She didn't give them a chance to tell her the results of their search for clues. Instead, she hurried them inside to deliver the bad news.

"Where's Charlie?" Sandy looked out across the darkening yard before she closed the kitchen door.

"Unsaddling the horses," Kirstie explained. She took off her slicker and left it dripping in the porch. "What are you saying—Matt found out about Cadillac and Crazy Horse?"

Making the girls sit by the stove while she fixed a hot drink, her mom nodded. "I just had him on the phone before you got back. He was pretty mad, looking for someone to blame. I had to get him to cool down; said what were we gonna do, have someone guard the remuda every second of the day and night? He took the point. Then he got real upset." Sandy faltered and sighed as she mixed the hot chocolate. "It kinda sank in slowly, I guess. He asked me over and over, were we sure it was Cadillac and Crazy Horse?"

"Jeez!" Kirstie pictured her brother making the phone call from a pay phone on the college campus. All her efforts to persuade her mother not to tell Matt about the horses had come to nothing, after all.

"How did Matt find out?" Lisa wanted to know as the door handle turned, and Charlie followed them into the room. The wrangler came forward for his mug of hot chocolate, unaware of what had happened.

Silently, Sandy handed over the drink.

"Mom, how did Matt hear the bad news?" Kirstie insisted.

Charlie stared at her, then retreated two or three quick steps into the corner of the room. Kirstie and Lisa followed his movement in the gathering silence.

"Oh, gee!" The young wrangler's jaw dropped as Kirstie, Lisa, and Sandy stared at him. "You mean, Matt had no idea...?"

"You told him!" Kirstie stood up, eyes wide, voice strained and high.

"Hush, Kirstie!" Sandy warned.

"How? When? Why?" She advanced toward Charlie in disbelief.

"I called him earlier today. I thought he knew. I left a message for him to call me back when he came out of his exam, said I wanted to talk with him about Cadillac and Crazy Horse going missing..." Charlie tailed off and took a deep breath. It came out again as a loud, helpless sigh.

"Why?" Kirstie repeated. "Didn't you know we wanted to keep it from him?"

"Obviously not." Sandy stepped in between Charlie and Kirstie. "How could he? Charlie isn't a mind reader. He wasn't in the room when we talked about it, so how could we expect him to realize that we were keeping the theft a secret so that Matt wouldn't come rushing home?"

"I wanted to tell him I was sorry," he said quietly, head down, staring at the brown and cream patterned rug, the parallel lines of the polished floorboards beyond. "He's my buddy. I thought it must be tough for him not having anyone to talk to over there in Denver."

"Poor Matt." It was Kirstie's turn to gasp and sigh. She understood in a flash that Charlie had called her brother because he was a good friend. "Sorry, Charlie. I wasn't thinking straight."

"Yeah, but I feel bad," he told them, managing to look up from the floor at last. "What did Matt say he was gonna do?"

Sandy closed her eyes and screwed up her mouth, leaning one hand on the table for support. "He didn't make much sense," she admitted. "He was like you, Kirstie: he was more afraid about what'll happen to Crazy Horse. He could see the point of stealing Cadillac, but..."

"OK!" Kirstie cut her mom short. "I know! But

Matt doesn't plan to come home, does he? You told him there isn't anything he can do?"

"Yes." Sandy Scott pulled herself upright again. "He wanted to jump right into his car and drive out here, of course. But I told him Larry Francini knows all about it, and we're doing every single thing we can to get those horses back."

"So?" Kirstie knew her brother's impetuous nature all too well. He matched her for hot-headed decisions more often than not. She imagined him, headlights glaring, speeding along Route 3 through San Luis, down the five miles of dirt road to the ranch right this minute.

"So, in the end, he agreed to stay in town," Sandy told them. "He'll take his exam tomorrow."

"He promised?" Kirstie double-checked.

Sandy nodded and moved briskly to take away the empty mugs from the table.

"But who knows if he'll stick to his promise?" she concluded quietly, as Charlie backed awkwardly out of the room onto the porch and Lisa went to call her mom for a lift home.

"Maybe he will," Kirstie whispered back as she

stared out of the window at the dark horizon. "I guess all we can do is wait and see."

"Well, there ain't a whole lot of information to go on," Sheriff Francini drawled when Kirstie came into his Main Street office early next morning. She'd put the coil of rope down on his desk and told him where they'd picked it up. Then she'd asked if his investigation into the theft of the two horses had made any progress.

"Did you check the local saddlery store?" She reminded him about the fancy red and white bridle—the one detail about the rustlers that might prove useful.

"Yup. Nothing," he replied shortly. "Ain't no local source for plaited bridles. You see them advertised in *American Cowboy* magazine every now and then, most likely made way out in California. A bridle like that comes pretty darned expensive."

"California?" Kirstie frowned. She opened her mouth to make the connection between Wes Logan and his ranch at Bluebird Hill, then shut it quickly. Even she had enough sense to realize that Sheriff Francini would call it coincidence—a long shot not worth considering. Better keep quiet and store it carefully inside her own head.

Larry Francini stood up and eased the silver buckle of his belt where it had pressed against his ample waistline. "We're pretty much looking at a stone wall," he confessed, picking up his white Stetson. "You kids are doing a good job picking up a clue like this fancy rope on Hummingbird Rock, but I wouldn't let it get your hopes up too high."

"Why not?" Kirstie had visited the sheriff on her way to school. Glancing at her watch, she realized she had to hurry to make her first class of the morning.

Sheriff Francini was also on his way somewhere. He led her out onto the street, where his car was parked. "You want my theory," he said with quiet confidentiality, "we're looking at professional horse rustlers here, not local amateurs. I heard last week about a gang from the south, moving north through the state."

Kirstie listened hard. "Do you know who they are?"

"Nope. They're too smart to get caught so far. Four or five of them. They hit and move on. Took three horses from a ranch in Idaho a couple of weeks back, then five from a place in Arizona. Now it's Colorado and your bad luck to be a target."

Sighing and saying good-bye, she wondered if he could be right. Turning to the car, she asked the sheriff one last important question. "What do these rustlers do with the stolen horses?"

Larry Francini leaned out of the car to answer. "They drive 'em out of the neighborhood while it's still dark; maybe south to New Mexico, to one of the big sale barns there."

"They sell them?" It made her blood run cold to think of Cadillac and Crazy Horse being prodded and poked by indifferent buyers.

"Sure. No questions asked. These guys make a fast buck and move on to the next hit." Looking her straight in the eye, Sheriff Francini delivered his best advice. "Listen, kid, forget it. Put it down to bad luck, move on. OK?"

His car was in gear, cruising away from the curb as he spoke. Kirstie watched him go. Forget it? Move on? With Crazy Horse likely to be sold for dog meat? With Cadillac split up from his best friend, pining for home? Forget it...no way!

\* \* \*

The school day had never been longer, classes never such a drag. Kirstie willed herself to concentrate and failed. Instead of algebra, she thought of Matt riding Cadillac by the side of Eden Lake on a spring day, blue columbines carpeting the meadow at the lakeside. Or she saw Matt on Crazy Horse, loping a figure eight, performing a sliding halt in thirty feet, spinning on the spot.

"Hey, Kirstie." Lisa met her at the school gates at the end of the day. "You wanna ride out to Lazy B on Lucky and Jitterbug? Maybe we could pick up a couple more clues."

Kirstie nodded. "Thanks, Lisa. Let's give it another shot."

They sat together on the school bus, which dropped them off at the turnoff to Half Moon Ranch, then hitched a ride with Smiley Gilpin, the forest guard, in his national forest jeep, reaching the ranch without having to call Sandy to drive out to meet them on the dirt road.

Smiley dropped them off at the gates and watched them down the first few yards of the steep driveway, then revved his engine and drove on. As they walked, the girls discussed the route they might take over

Miners' Ridge, down into the next valley. This time they would choose a right turn along the side of Horseshoe Creek to Jim Mullins's ranch.

It was only when they drew within fifty yards of the ranch house itself that Kirstie looked up and paid any attention to her surroundings. It was a quarter after four on a dull, gray day, dirty snow on the ground, the ranch-house chimney smoking, the kitchen door swinging open…

"No!" Kirstie let out a sudden groan. There, parked close against the porch steps, was a pale blue, beaten-up car. Its fender was bent and hanging off, the body was dented and deeply encrusted with dirt.

"That's Matt's car!" Lisa gasped. She stood still and let Kirstie run ahead.

"What happened? Where's Matt?" Kirstie flew into the house to find her mom sitting at the kitchen table, staring into space. "Did he skip his exam?"

Sandy took a long time to look around. "No, he took the test. But he wants to quit college."

Kirstie took a deep breath. She couldn't look her mom in the eye.

"You knew?" Sandy stared accusingly at Kirstie.

"I didn't...I wasn't sure."

"You suspected?"

"Mom, what happened? Where's Matt now?"

"Charlie tried to talk to him, but he stormed off."

"Let me try. Where did he go?"

"I don't know. But honey, it's no use. The mood he's in, Matt won't listen to anyone!"

Kirstie found her brother sitting on the fence of Red Fox Meadow, his back to the ranch, facing the herd of horses feeding from the racks of hay that Charlie had just delivered.

There were Lucky and Rodeo Rocky, the inseparable twosome of the palomino and the bay. There was dainty, skittish Jitterbug, and solid, easygoing Moose. Johnny Mohawk broke from the group and galloped the length of the field for the heck of it, his black mane and tail flying, his hooves kicking up frozen snow.

"Hey," Kirstie said quietly as she climbed the fence to join Matt.

He blinked without turning his head, his gaze fixed on the black horse.

Something in his posture told Kirstie how much he was hurting. His shoulders were hunched, his hands gripping the top rail of the fence. "I'm sorry," she whispered.

He seemed to be staring at the herd, trying to believe that Cadillac and Crazy Horse were still there, that this whole thing had been a terrible mistake...

But there was no sleek, white gelding challenging the black half-Arab to a race, no light brown, stumpy-legged follower clowning along at his partner's heels.

"It's true, isn't it?" he muttered. His face was pale with shock, his eyes dark.

Though he would deny it, would rant and rave and go crazy with anger rather than admit it, she could see his heart was broken. Slowly, painfully, she began to tell him the whole story.

**7**

It was forty-eight hours since Crazy Horse and Cadillac had been stolen.

The family had talked through the crisis all through Tuesday evening, helping Matt to come to terms with the loss of his two horses, looking at his future as calmly as they could.

"I want you to graduate as a vet," Sandy Scott had told him. "Whatever you think now, however badly you feel, I still want you to finish college."

He'd said it was waste of time, his heart wasn't in it, he wanted to work at Half Moon Ranch to take some of the load off her.

"If Dad was around to help, like he should be, I wouldn't feel this way," Matt had insisted.

Kirstie's own heart had been squeezed when he said that. *If Dad hadn't left us...if he hadn't found a new woman, a new life...*

"But he isn't," Sandy had said emptily, finally.

"Then it's up to me. I've gotta do it!" Matt had brought the argument full circle.

They'd reached a compromise. Matt had said he had one and a half days before his next exam. Sandy had agreed he could stay at home until then, help in the search for Cadillac and Crazy Horse, then drive back to Denver to finish the tests.

"After that, we'll talk again," she insisted. "Short-term, you can stick around. I understand you need to do everything you can to find the horses. And Kirstie, me, Charlie, and Hadley, we'll all do our bit to help get them back. But long-term, we're not deciding anything right now. OK?"

Grudgingly, Matt had agreed.

"Thirty-six hours!" Kirstie sighed now as she went to her bedroom window and looked out across the meadow. "Forty-eight since it happened. Thirty-six to mend Matt's broken heart."

The moon shone bright in a clear sky. The whole valley was lit by a weird silver light that picked out the shapes of the cabins on the hillside, the stands of aspen trees, the jagged horizons.

In Red Fox Meadow, the horses stood still and alert. They were listening.

Kirstie opened her window and leaned out. She saw the horses lift their heads and turn their faces in the direction of Five Mile Creek.

An indistinct figure appeared on the bank of the river. It plodded slowly, unevenly, toward the ranch, emerging from shadowy trees, weaving unsteadily and sometimes losing its footing to plunge knee-deep into the icy water. Then the horse would stagger, regain his balance, climb up the bank, and walk slowly on.

Flinging on a jacket and boots, flying downstairs, Kirstie ran out of the house. The door banged against the wall, her feet clattered on the wooden deck, then she was plunging into the dark, racing for the footbridge, gasping for breath as she sprinted to meet the weary traveler.

"Crazy Horse!" She wrapped her arms around his neck. He lowered his big, ugly-beautiful head.

The pale, tan horse was quivering from head to foot. His coat was caked with mud, his blond mane matted and tangled. And there was a burn mark on his neck where a rope had tightened and rubbed—a long, open sore that had cut through the skin, bled, and congealed.

"Oh, gosh, where have you been?" Kirstie gasped. "What did they do to you?"

He shook his head free, walked on doggedly toward the house.

Matt appeared in the doorway, his lean figure silhouetted in a square of yellow lamplight. For a moment, he stood stock-still. Then he sprang toward Kirstie and Crazy Horse. Across the yard, a light came on in the bunkhouse. The door opened, and first Hadley, then Charlie came out to see what was going on.

It was Matt that Crazy Horse needed to see. He staggered with Kirstie as far as the corral, where his owner stood, stopping again in disbelief, looking from one to the other and eventually walking slowly toward the horse.

Matt reached out to touch Crazy Horse's cheek. The horse leaned his head toward him, his eyelids drooped, he breathed a long, drawn-out sigh.

"He must have walked miles!" Sandy Scott was as overjoyed as Matt and Kirstie at the return of the steadfast horse. She'd lifted his legs and examined his feet, found them cut and sore, the shoes packed with dirt and sharp stones.

Hadley had told Matt to take Crazy Horse into the stable and bed him down on fresh straw. The old ranch hand advised drink but no feed until the exhausted horse had begun to recover from his ordeal.

"You're so smart!" Kirstie drew a blanket over his back. "You worked out a way to escape and came all the way home!"

Crazy Horse stood in his stall, head lowered, still shivering under the warm blanket.

"How far do you reckon he traveled?" Charlie wanted to know as he raked more straw into a comfortable bed. "To me, it looks like he walked a heck of a long way."

"Who knows?" Sandy was taking a closer look at the rope burn on Crazy Horse's neck. "Maybe I'd better call Glen Woodford," she muttered.

But Matt stepped in. He examined the broken skin and asked Charlie to fetch water and soft, clean cotton rags. "It's a superficial cut," he explained calmly. "Our problem is dirt around the wound. I'll clean it up and use antiseptic cream. Let's keep an eye on his temperature. If it shoots up by morning, we'll know there's an infection that needs to be treated with antibiotics. That's when we bring in a qualified vet."

Kirstie watched her brother work on the wound as he talked. She saw Crazy Horse quiver as Matt rubbed the dirt out of the wound and reached

out to soothe him by stroking his nose and cheek. "You're a hero!" she whispered. "A star!"

"Maybe." Hadley broke into her imagined picture of how it must have been, of Crazy Horse defying his captors to break loose and escape. "Then again, maybe the rustlers dumped him."

Charlie took him up. "You mean, once he'd served his purpose of luring Cadillac out of Red Fox Meadow, they drove till it was safe, then let him go?"

The old wrangler nodded tersely. "More trouble than it was worth to truck him down to a sale barn."

Kirstie frowned. "What do they know?" She stroked and hugged and made a fuss of the brave horse. But mention of Cadillac had distracted her. She sidled up to Matt, who was working white cream into Crazy Horse's neck wound with gentle, circular movements of his fingertips. "Now that he's back safe, it just leaves us with the problem of finding Cadillac," she murmured.

He nodded.

"I was thinking about it and came up with a plan."

"Which is?" The urgency in Matt's voice made her whisper.

"I'm gonna do what Sheriff Francini should have done right away, and that's call around all the sale barns."

"To ask if anyone has tried to sell Cadillac?"

To Kirstie, this sounded good. "He's a pretty unusual horse. The sale-barn managers are bound to spot him."

Matt put the top on the tub of cream, then wiped his hands. "I don't care if I have to call every horse sale barn in the country; if that's what it takes, I'm gonna do it!"

It was Hadley again who put in the warning note. "Maybe it ain't gonna be that easy. You're supposing that every guy in every sale barn is a regular, honest joe: you ask them a question, they give you a straight answer."

"Why would they lie?" Kirstie demanded. "If a manager learns that Cadillac's been stolen, won't he turn him over to the cops?"

Hadley's thin, wrinkled face creased into a look of stubborn doubt. "Not if there's a few thousand dollars resting on the deal and a good percentage to the guy who runs the sale."

"You saying we shouldn't even bother to

call?" Matt was winding himself up, ready to argue.

Sandy wanted everyone to leave Crazy Horse's stall so that the exhausted horse could get some sleep. Matt's raised voice was disturbing him. She ushered them all out into the passageway and turned out the light.

"I'm saying be glad Crazy Horse made it," Hadley insisted. He led the way out into the dark corral.

"And forget about Cadillac?" Matt challenged.

"You got one horse back. I'd guess that was one more than was likely." The wrangler's gravelly voice refused to back down. "And those guys had plans for the pedigree before they even rustled him— plans that they ain't about to let you spoil."

Kirstie turned to appeal to her mom. "We're not gonna listen to that!"

"We're paying attention," Sandy said steadily. She nodded good night to Charlie and Hadley, then headed inside the house. As Kirstie careered in after her, falling over herself in her rush to protest, her mom turned around and took her firmly by the shoulders. "I can't dismiss what Hadley just said. After all, he's been

101

around sale barns all his life. He knows what he's saying."

"But…C-Cadillac…!" Kirstie stammered.

Sandy nodded. "I know. I want him back as much as you and Matt." Pausing to think ahead, rubbing her forehead, she finally decided what they should do. "Matt, you make those phone calls first thing in the morning. We owe it to poor Cadillac to at least try!"

Crazy Horse stood in Red Fox Meadow in the golden-pink dawn light. He stared wistfully down the length of the long, white fence toward the mountains, looking as if he expected Cadillac's solitary, graceful figure to appear.

"Where is he, Crazy Horse? Where's Cadillac?" Kirstie whispered. The fresh air, the wide open space calmed her after a disturbed night's sleep. She'd left her mom in the kitchen making coffee, and Matt making a list of all the sale barns he could find in the phone book. "You know where Cadillac is, if only you could tell us!"

Before he attacked the phone book, Matt had been out to the stable to take Crazy Horse's temperature. "Normal," he reported. "No infection. And he wants out," he told Sandy, still in her robe, yawning as she came downstairs. "He's leaning over the door of the stall, yelling at the top of his voice to be allowed out into the meadow."

"I know. I heard him whinnying. In fact, he woke me up." Sandy had agreed that Crazy Horse knew best. "If he feels up to it after his adventure, and you're satisfied he's OK, Matt, put him out."

Kirstie had seen her brother's face color as he realized that their mom was trusting his judgment without calling in Glen Woodford. He'd walked tall out of the house to take Crazy Horse to the remuda. And he'd grinned at Kirstie, who'd scrambled into her school clothes and run out to join him.

Now, after he'd gone back to the house with a new spring in his stride, she drank in the quiet scene: the green grass showing through patches of melted snow in the meadow, the horses munching at the hayrack, Crazy Horse standing by the fence, one sore foot lifted clear of the ground, looking longingly into the distance…

\*    \*    \*

The sound of the phone ringing inside the house made Kirstie quicken her pace as she returned from the remuda for breakfast. Who could it be so early?

"Larry Francini," Sandy told her, one hand over the mouthpiece. "Matt's upstairs in his room. Run and get him, please!"

Kirstie rushed to pass on the message, but by the time they both got back to the kitchen, their mom was already off the phone.

"Never underestimate the county sheriff!" she told them, her gray eyes alive, a smile twitching at the corners of her mouth. "Larry may look like your average guy who couldn't put two and two together, but he just came up with something good!"

"Anything to do with the fancy rope and bridle?" Kirstie asked. This was clearly good news. Sandy was lifting newspapers and magazines off the windowsill, searching for a pen and a piece of paper to write on.

"Nope. Actually something about this place!" She scribbled down a name and number and showed them.

Kirstie narrowed her eyes to read the scrawl. "Columbine Falls Sale Barn—970-555-0929."

"What is it?" Matt snatched the paper. "Why has Sheriff Francini given you this?"

Sandy's smile broadened. "He got there before us, Matt. He said he'd spent yesterday evening calling the barns to the south of here to see if there was a horse like Cadillac going through the sales. He drew blanks. Then, late last night, a call came through. The caller had heard he was asking questions, said he had a mystery tip-off, if the sheriff wanted to hear it."

Matt listened and nodded. "Saying what, exactly?"

"Telling him that a gray gelding fitting Cadillac's description had been located at Columbine Falls Sale Barn in southwest Colorado."

"Let's go!" Matt's reaction was instantaneous. He reached for his jacket and hat. "The Falls is 200 miles from here; that's a three-hour drive. C'mon, Mom, let's get moving!"

Sandy steadied him. "According to the tip-off, the horse is scheduled to be put through a sale early this afternoon. That gives us plenty of time to go down and identify him."

Matt nodded. "What about Sheriff Francini?"

"He's not coming. He's been in contact with the

county sheriff down there, fixed up for us to meet him at midday." All was organized and in order, Sandy gave them to understand. But even she couldn't hide her excitement.

"What about me? Can I come?" Kirstie begged. She didn't want to miss the big moment when Matt walked into the sale barn to claim his horse.

"You've got school!" her mom reminded her. No arguments, no softening under pressure.

And so a silent, pale, frowning Kirstie was dropped off at the gates of San Luis Middle School at eight-thirty that morning. She'd pleaded and reasoned to no effect. "No way, Kirstie!" Sandy had stood firm. "School is important. Matt and I can do this without your help!"

Left out in the cold, overlooked and rejected; that was how she felt when Lisa came up to her in the school yard. Her mom and brother would be away all day, reclaiming the stolen horse. They'd have all the joy and relief, all the pleasure of a great reunion.

"Why the black looks?" Lisa quizzed. "No one died, did they?"

"Nope." Kirstie walked on ahead, chopping her replies, taking it out on Lisa.

"What then?"

"Crazy Horse came home."

"Hey, Kirstie, that's great!...So how come you're not over the moon?" Lisa ran in front of her to intercept her.

"And they found Cadillac!" she snapped, sidestepping into the classroom. "At least, they think they did. In some sale barn in the south. That's where Mom and Matt are driving right this very minute!"

**8**

Lisa twisted her plaited friendship bracelet, working herself up to a big statement. "Being your friend means a lot to me," she told Kirstie. "But I guess to you, it doesn't mean as much."

"How do you figure that out?" Kirstie blushed. Though she stood in line for the school bus to take her home at the end of the day, her mind was elsewhere. *Had Mom and Matt gotten to the sale barn in time?* she wondered. Was it truly Cadillac that the mystery caller had spotted?

"If *I* was in *your* place, I wouldn't shut *me* out."
Lisa's sentence came out all mixed up. "Not like
you did all during today!"

"Like when?" The yellow bus drew up. Kids began
to climb in.

"Like when I saw you in the yard this morning.
Like when you went by in the corridor at break.
Like now, for instance!"

Kirstie reached the front of the line. "Look, I'm
sorry, OK? I've got a lot of stress."

"Right! Which is why you need me!" Lisa's green
eyes flashed angrily at the boy behind Kirstie, who
shoved them aside so he could get on the bus.
"That's what friends are for!"

Kirstie sighed. She knew Lisa was right.

"Are you girls getting on this bus or not?" the driver
called, ready to press the button and close the door.

"Yes!" Like it or not, Kirstie had to leave the
tricky situation with Lisa and get home fast. She
wanted to be there when Matt and her mother got
back with Cadillac.

"No need." Lisa had spotted Charlie's car cruising down Main Street. He'd waved and hollered
to offer them a ride.

So the bus pulled away, and the young wrangler's car took its place at the curb. "And before you ask, no news from Matt so far," he told Kirstie as she climbed in. "You coming, Lisa?"

Lisa stooped to peer in at Kirstie. "Am I?"

"Yeah, I need to talk. And jeez, Lisa, I'm sorry I've been such a jerk."

"That's OK." Relieved, she settled into the back seat beside Kirstie. "So, tell me!"

Charlie drove as Kirstie talked. She described the magic moment when Crazy Horse came back, the surprise call from Sheriff Francini, the way her mom had cut her out, sent her to school, and how much that had hurt.

"But you know how she is about Matt and college," Lisa reminded her. "It's the same with you and school. You gotta be there."

"I guess." Kirstie frowned. She still hadn't confessed what was really on her mind. "You know what? Matt was so happy this morning. The news about the sale barn came through, and you should've seen him. He could hardly wait to get out of the house."

"So?" Lisa indicated that it was understandable. "How would you be? You just found out where your favorite horse in the whole world is. You're gonna be 'up'!"

"But I've had time to think since then," Kirstie went on, noticing Charlie look at her in his rearview mirror. "Maybe we reacted too quick. We hear about a white horse for sale in the Falls, we jump right in there. But what if this horse isn't Cadillac?"

Charlie heard and swerved slightly in the road. Lisa groaned. "Oh, my!"

"Right." Kirstie waited for the doubt to sink in. "How's Matt gonna feel if he drives 200 miles just to find out it's a false lead?"

Kirstie got the strong feeling that Crazy Horse agreed with her. He was at the white fence when Charlie's car pulled into the yard, trotting up and down to attract their attention, limping slightly on his sore foot. When Kirstie, Lisa, and Charlie got out of the car, the sturdy tan horse threw back his heavy head, curled his lip, and whinnied loudly.

"If only he could talk," Charlie said quietly. He stood, thumbs hooked into the back pockets of his jeans, staring at Crazy Horse. "He could sure tell us everything we need to know!"

Charlie had echoed Kirstie's feeling from earlier that day. It made her drift thoughtfully across the bridge toward Red Fox Meadow. "Maybe he can talk...kinda."

"Talk...how?" Lisa climbed and sat astride the fence, turning her collar up against the stiff, cold wind blowing down from the mountains. "Like, he's gonna tell us what happened Sunday night?"

"Horses talk," Kirstie insisted. "Leastways, they communicate. They use body language."

Lisa studied Crazy Horse. "He *is* kinda jumpy. Restless. Look at his ears!"

The horse carried his head high and flicked his ears. There was tension running through his body, making him swish his tail and stamp his feet as he trotted and turned.

"I'd say he's trying to tell us something, no doubt about it," Kirstie insisted. "But he knows we're stupid, so he's having to wait for us to figure it out."

"It's about Cadillac." Lisa grew convinced. She retraced recent events to try to understand Crazy Horse's impatience. "He's taken prisoner by a bunch of rustlers. They treat him and Cadillac rough. He escapes. Then what does he do? He heads for home. He wants to tell us about Cadillac, his buddy—where he is, what these guys are planning to do to him. Only we take no notice. We stick him in a field and leave him. No wonder he's upset!"

That was it; Lisa's clear version of the story made Kirstie come to a decision. She swung her leg over the fence and jumped into the field, took hold of Crazy Horse's head collar, and led him toward the gate. "Find Charlie!" she called. "Ask him to bring two saddles to the corral."

"Who for?" Lisa held the gate steady as the wind caught it. Her eyes were lit up, her movements quick and excited.

"For Lucky and Crazy Horse." Kirstie's mind was made up. "We can't hang around doing nothing. We gotta follow Crazy Horse. So long as we trust him, he'll tell us everything we need to know!"

Charlie had argued the sensible case: wait until your mom and Matt get home, until the bad weather passes over, until Crazy Horse's lame foot clears up.

113

But Kirstie and Lisa had got it into their heads; it must be now, there could be no delay. "We waited long enough to start listening to Crazy Horse," Kirstie told the young wrangler. "He's been wearing himself out in that meadow trying to make us listen to him."

"We'll be back in a couple of hours," Lisa promised. "We're carrying a radio to call you if we hit trouble."

"And you call us if Mom and Matt get back," Kirstie reminded him. Crazy Horse was saddled and tacked up, straining at the reins to head out toward Miners' Ridge.

"You take care," Charlie warned. "Stick to the trail—remember, Crazy Horse has been through a tough time already."

They set off with his cautious words in their ears, across the creek to pick up Meltwater Trail out of the valley. Crazy Horse trotted ahead of Lisa and Lucky, testing his sore foot and soon breaking into a lope. He ducked his head and settled into a steady stride, his pale mane streaming back, hooves thundering over the frozen earth.

"His foot doesn't seem to bother him so much

when he's loping!" Kirstie called back to Lisa. She dodged sideways to miss the sticking-out branch of a lodgepole pine, regained her balance, and let her horse lope on.

...Up the slope between the trees, toward the heavy clouds clinging to the mountain peaks... Past Hummingbird Rock...They retraced the route that the rustlers had dragged Crazy Horse along on Sunday night.

"He sure knows where he's headed!" Lisa gasped when both horses came to a crashing stream and were forced to slow down. She shouted above the noise of the tumbling, splashing water. "Lucky's having a hard time keeping up!"

Once more, Kirstie gave Crazy Horse his head and let him cross the stream where he chose. She felt his shoulders dip as he descended the steep, rock-strewn bank. She leaned back in the saddle, felt the icy water splash her legs and soak through her jeans. "Here comes the snow!" she warned Lisa as the wind cut through her jacket and the first flakes began to fall.

It drove down from the gray sky in flurries, the giant flakes soft as feathers, cold as ice, cutting down visibility so that Kirstie and Lisa could soon see no farther than the next tree. The horses had struggled through the stream and carried on, heads down, trudging higher until they came to a narrow gully called Fat Man's Squeeze. Here, sheer rocks rose to either side. The wind drove the snow furiously through the channel, whirling it into the girls' faces and forcing their eyes almost shut.

For a second, halfway through the squeeze, Crazy Horse hesitated. Snow caked his mane and eyelashes, his feet slid on the packed ice, the wind blasted him full in the face.

"Keep going!" Lisa yelled. Lucky was hard on Crazy Horse's heels. If they stopped now, there was no room to turn and go back.

Kirstie kicked hard with her heels. "C'mon, boy; you can make it!"

The brave horse shook the loose snow from his mane and plunged on. Slowly, painfully, he emerged through the far end of Fat Man's Squeeze.

And then they were on Miners' Ridge. Kirstie recognized the ancient mounds of mine waste, the eerie, boarded-up entrances to long-disused shafts.

"Narrow trail ahead!" she yelled over her shoulder. "Keep to the left!"

On their right, invisible in the blizzard, was a sheer drop into Dead Man's Canyon. Crazy Horse and Lucky knew the path well, and instinct told them to steer clear of the cliff. They slowed their pace to a crawl, one foot after another, listening to the rattle of loose stones falling over the edge and peppering into the canyon a hundred feet below.

*Trust your horse!* Kirstie repeated the phrase to herself under her breath. It was the Half Moon Ranch mantra—the phrase they taught to visitors on their first day's ride. *Trust your horse.* If you followed the basic rule, you'd be safe.

Her fingers were so stiff with cold she could hardly hold the reins, her whole body was rigid and numb. But she pressed on. "You OK?" she yelled back to Lisa.

"Nope!" The reply was whipped away by the wind. "But me and Lucky, we'll cowboy-up!"

The blizzard lasted ten minutes. As quickly as it came, it was gone. The wind died down, the snowflakes eased, then stopped completely. All around, there was a white wonderland of freshly fallen snow.

Though the trail was covered and the branches of trees sagged with the weight of the snow, Crazy Horse ploughed smoothly on. He crested the mountain and picked his way down the far slope across Lazy B land. A willing follower, Lucky carried Lisa in his wake.

"Hey, Kirstie, shouldn't we call Charlie to tell him we're OK?" Lisa shouted. "That snowstorm will hit Half Moon Ranch soon. He's gonna wonder if we made it."

Fumbling in the pocket of her slicker with ice-cold fingers, Kirstie reached for her radio and made the call. When Charlie answered, she gave him their position: "Half a mile from Horseshoe Creek," she reported. "Crazy Horse found his way through the storm. Now he's picking up his pace, heading straight for the river. Over."

"Gotcha, Kirstie. No message from your mom and Matt this end. Over."

She listened hard to understand the message through the mush and crackle caused by the weak signal. "OK, Charlie. We'll keep in touch." Signing off, she slipped the radio back into her pocket and sat tight until they reached the creek.

"Which way now?" Lisa muttered. She gazed around at the snow falling gently from nearby branches, letting them spring back into position. Across the stream, a mottled, gray bobcat broke cover from under a fallen tree trunk and stole silently up the bank, its footprints clear in the smooth snow.

"Over the bridge," Kirstie whispered. She felt Crazy Horse watch the bobcat on its way, then set off determinedly across the rough planks.

"Onto Ponderosa Pines land!" Lisa sounded worried but not surprised. "Are we sure we want to do this?"

"We don't have a choice." *Trust your horse*, Kirstie repeated to herself. Crazy Horse was certain that this was the way he wanted to go.

They continued along the bank toward Wes Logan's ranch house, bushwhacking across country, through trees, over open land until the house and stables came into view.

"Déjà vu!" Lisa groaned. Her teeth chattered, she

sat hunched in the saddle, trying to joke to hide her unease. "Didn't we already come this route once before?"

"It looks deserted," Kirstie said, "except for the horse box in the yard." But Crazy Horse was more eager than ever to go on, not caring who saw them from the windows of the ranch house. She had to let him walk on, only reining him back again when they came to the final stand of bare aspens between them and the house.

"Whoa!" She ordered Crazy Horse to stop. "I mean it; whoa, boy!"

He tossed his head and strained against her. Why wouldn't she let him carry on? There was something down there that he needed to show her.

But Kirstie slipped from the saddle and led him, protesting, toward the nearest tree. "This is as far as you go," she told him firmly, hitching the lead rope around a low branch. "You leave the rest to us, you hear?"

Crazy Horse snorted and stamped his feet. He let her know he objected to the tether.

"Ssh!" Lisa pleaded. She, too, tied Lucky to a tree. "Give us a break, you...*crazy horse!*"

"Wait here!" Kirstie repeated. "We're gonna creep down on foot, take a secret look, OK?"

Up went the head with a toss of the pale mane. He strained at the rope in protest.

"Let's go!" Lisa said. "If we're gonna do this, let's do it!"

So they left the uneasy horses hidden in the trees and made for Wes Logan's stable block, dodging from rock to rock, holding their breath, peering out at the house, edging forward again.

"Hold it!" Kirstie put out an arm to stop Lisa. She made her duck down behind a snowdrift by a fence twenty or thirty yards from the stable. A door was swinging slowly open, a man was leading out a white horse.

"It's Logan!" Lisa gasped. "And...and..."

"San Luis Dawn!" For one, two, maybe three seconds, Kirstie's heart was in her mouth. The horse was wearing red leg and tail bandages, as if for a journey; an exact match for Cadillac, but female, she realized as the rancher led her out toward the horse box. "Today must be the day they drive her to California!"

"For a moment there, I thought it was Cadillac!"

Lisa swallowed hard. Disappointment was written all over her face.

"But look! Look at the head collar!" Kirstie kept hold of her friend's arm, gripped it tight. San Luis Dawn was wearing expensive, fancy tack. It was made from red and white plaited leather, with a lead rope to match.

"Wait till we tell the sheriff!" Forgetting how scared she'd been, Lisa grinned at Kirstie. "That's why Crazy Horse brought us back here, isn't it? So we could pick up evidence like this to link Wes Logan with the rustlers!"

Kirstie nodded. "But it's not over yet. I know in my bones there's more!"

Crouching, listening, waiting, they saw Wes Logan steady the gray mare and bring her to a halt by the ramp leading into the box. But the horse began to act up, and they heard him shout for help, saw another man come quickly out of the stable. Between them, the two men attempted to lead the mare inside the horse box.

Lisa and Kirstie held on until Logan and his helper had the horse halfway up the ramp.

"Now!" Kirstie whispered. She crawled under the

fence and sprinted for the stable. There was a side door out of sight of the men at work in the yard. It would give them a chance to scout around in secret and be out again before the rancher had San Luis Dawn safely tethered and ready for her trip.

The girls slid into the stable, breathed in the warm air, the sweet smell of hay and horse. They looked down the row of light, airy stalls, heard the unconcerned rustle of hay nets as horses in the stalls nibbled and munched.

"Wait!" It was Lisa's turn to hold Kirstie back. She pointed to a stall at the far end as a man emerged carrying more of the special tack that had given Wes Logan away. He walked quickly out of the main door and across the yard.

"That was close!" Kirstie admitted. She felt suddenly hot and breathless. And the horses in the stalls seemed to have sensed their presence. They grew restless, coming to poke their heads over their doors. Then they snorted and blew, rolling their eyes in alarm.

"*Too* close!" Lisa breathed. "C'mon, Kirstie, let's get out of here!"

"Not until I take a look in that stall." Kirstie's eyes

had narrowed. Gut feeling took over. Her life depended on being able to edge down the aisle until she could see into the stall at the end of the row.

Closer, closer…The men in the horse box exchanged a joke with the man in the yard. They laughed hoarsely. Lisa crept between the stalls after Kirstie. Then they reached the end and stood up straight.

There was a horse in there. An elegant, gray, beautiful horse with dark eyes and a flowing mane. This time, there could be no mistake.

"Cadillac!" Lisa gasped. She turned to Kirstie. "I knew it!"

"Me, too. It looks like he's been here all along."

Kirstie had to say it out loud to believe it. Taken by surprise, she felt she could hardly breathe or move a muscle. "That's what Crazy Horse has been trying to tell us!"

"So call Charlie. Tell him we found Cadillac!" Excitement raised Lisa's voice above a whisper. She reached into Kirstie's pocket to grab the radio. "Give me, give me!"

Inside his stall, the magnificent white horse thumped his hoof against the wooden boards.

Lisa pressed the on button. "Charlie! Charlie! It's Lisa. Come in, please!"

There was a crackle of static sound, no reply.

"Charlie!"

A gloved hand came down and sent the radio crashing to the floor. A figure loomed over them: a man in a sheepskin jacket and a dark brown Stetson who came out of nowhere and smashed the radio to pieces.

Lisa screamed.

Kirstie whirled away from Cadillac to see the man hook one arm around Lisa's neck and pull her against him. At the far end of the stable, Wes Logan and his two other men flung open the door.

**9**

Kirstie didn't dare to move. Out of the corner of her eye, she saw the man nearby tighten his stranglehold on Lisa.

Wes Logan strode toward her. He grabbed her by the arm and shoved her against Cadillac's stall.

"What the heck...?" The shortest and heaviest of the three ranch hands demanded an explanation.

"She's the kid from Half Moon Ranch." Logan glared at Kirstie. He ignored Lisa and the man who held her in his grip.

"Tell him to let her go!" Kirstie begged.

The rancher's expression didn't alter. "Do as she asks, Johnson," he said calmly.

Slowly, the man obeyed.

Kirstie waited until Lisa stood free of the man, then let herself breathe again. Her back to the stall, she reached out a hand to her friend, whose trembling fingers curled around it and clasped it hard.

"What now?" The stocky man closed the stable door and threw them back into semidarkness.

Lisa's grip on Kirstie's hand tightened.

Inside the cramped space of the stall, Cadillac turned uneasily.

"You give us back our horse," Kirstie said. She had nothing to lose by confronting Logan. In spite of the threatening looks from the four men who surrounded them, there was no way the thieves could get away with this now that they'd been caught red-handed.

"*Your* horse?" Logan echoed.

"Yes. Cadillac belongs to my brother, Matt!"

"Cadillac?" The rancher shrugged as if confused. "You talking about the horse behind you?"

"Yes, and you know it!" This wasn't funny, though

the three men backing Logan up seemed to think so. "This is a Half Moon Ranch horse!"

Slowly, Logan shook his head. His men sneered as he talked. "No way. This horse belongs to me. I bought him from a ranch over in Montana two days ago. His name's Phantom."

"That's not true!" Kirstie stood clear of the wooden boards behind her. She knew the long, sleek lines of Cadillac's face, the curve of his neck as he arched it and thrust his head over the door of the stall. "You made that whole story up to cover your tracks!"

Logan kept his gaze steady. "His name's Phantom," he repeated. "I paid six thousand dollars for him to make him a pair with San Luis Dawn. Johnson and Gibb are all set to drive them both down to sunny California."

Kirstie shook her head fiercely. "You're lying!"

For the first time Logan allowed himself a brief, unpleasant smile. "Prove it," he said as he gestured for the man in the sheepskin coat and the heavy ranch hand to go into the stall and bring the horse out.

"We'll tell the cops!" Desperate to stop them, Kirstie threw caution to the winds.

"Kirstie, keep quiet!" Lisa squeezed her hand until it hurt.

Logan shoved them both to one side as Johnson seized the gray horse's lead rope. The horse reared and pulled away, but the man jerked hard on the rope to bring him into line. "Say what you like!" Logan snapped. "Who they gonna believe?"

"Us, because we're telling the truth!" Kirstie pulled away from Lisa. "Sheriff Francini knows all about the case. We told him about the plaited bridle; we even gave him a length of rope as a clue!"

"Oh, yeah, Larry Francini. He married my wife's cousin. We see them every Thanksgiving. I guess I can soon make him see what's going on around here. Yes, sir, I have to have a serious talk with him about you two trespassing on my land." Wes Logan was back to his smooth, sneering style.

Kicking and pulling, the gray horse emerged from the stall. He saw Kirstie and Lisa cowering in the corner, lifted his leg, and struck his hoof hard against the concrete floor.

"Just stand to one side, girls; give Phantom some room." Carelessly, the arrogant rancher issued orders.

Kirstie hated him. She loathed his smooth voice, his handsome, expressionless face.

The horse struck out again, almost twisting the rope from Johnson's hands.

But Gibb moved in to help, hooking a second lead rope to the horse's head collar. He held it short, and together, the two men dragged the horse out into the yard. The gray gelding kicked and strained as they forced him toward the ramp of the parked box.

"So what about the kids?" The third ranch hand, a dark-haired, long-faced man not much more than a kid himself, sounded anxious. "Do we let them go?"

"Not yet," Logan replied. "Let's get rid of the evidence first; wait until Johnson and Gibb get these horses down the road a way."

"So?" The nervous helper waited for orders from his boss.

Logan clicked his tongue while he considered a solution to the unexpected Kirstie and Lisa complication. He watched his men persuade the gray gelding up the ramp with knotted ropes which they beat against his flanks and withers. "So lock them in the tack room," he said briskly. "And scout around outside. Try to find out how they got all the way over to Ponderosa Pines."

Polished silver bits and fancy plaited bridles hung in a neat row. There were high-quality saddles sitting shiny and new on specially designed ledges in Wes Logan's well-equipped tack room.

Lisa sat down in one corner, head in hands.

"Liar!" Kirstie fumed. She stormed the length of the hut and back. "The guy's an out-and-out, dirty liar!"

"But smart." Lisa raised her head and sighed.

"He's right, Kirstie. We don't have enough hard evidence against him, so who's gonna believe us?"

"But that's Cadillac out there!" she protested. She went to the locked door, lay flat, and peered out through a chink. "We know it, they know it, we all know it!"

"Yeah, and once that truck heads west through the Rockies with the two horses inside, it's like Logan says: his word against ours!"

"He's a lousy, rotten horse thief!" Kirstie hissed. She could see the four men now. They checked that the white gelding was safe inside the horse box with San Luis Dawn. Then, leaving the ramp down, they crossed the yard and headed for the house.

"You boys will need maps, money for gas, the names of motels on the route," Logan was telling Gibb and Johnson. "And a cup of coffee before you set off." He led them onto the porch, around the corner, and out of sight.

"Can you believe that?" Kirstie beckoned for Lisa to join her. "The guy's so arrogant, he leaves us locked up in here and gives them coffee like he's got all the time in the world!"

Flat on her stomach, peering out under the tack-room door, Lisa was in time to see the men disappear. "Hey!" she said, suddenly jabbing Kirstie with her elbow. "Look who's here!"

Kirstie tilted her head and squinted to see where Lisa was pointing. There was just a narrow slit between the door and the wooden floor, and at first, all she could see was a set of hooves, sturdy white fetlocks, pale brown legs...

"Crazy Horse!" Lisa whispered. "He must have broken his tether!"

The horse limped across the snowy yard toward the horse box. He didn't waver or hesitate—he knew exactly where he was going.

"Oh...my...gosh!" Lisa breathed. She prayed that Logan and his men wouldn't come out of the house.

"He's seen the ramp...He's going up!" Kirstie watched with bated breath as more of Crazy Horse came into view. She could see the stirrups hanging loose from the saddle, the trailing rope, his heavy, mule-like face.

"They'll kill him if they see him!" Lisa jumped up and tried the door, even though she knew it was useless. The latch was fastened on the outside.

"He's inside the box!" Kirstie cried. "What a smart horse: see how easily he found Cadillac!"

Lisa rattled at the locked door. "Sure, I can hear that from way over here. And so can Logan!"

A shrill whinny echoed across the yard, then a loud answering call as the two horses were reunited.

"We gotta get out of here!" Kirstie joined Lisa. Together, they shoved hard against the door.

"No good!" Lisa dropped to her knees again to peer through the crack. "What's Crazy Horse up to now?"

The whinnies rose to a chorus of squeals. San Luis Dawn had joined in, too. The whole truck rocked and shook as the three horses jostled and stamped.

"I don't know for sure, but my guess is he's try-ing to set Cadillac free!" Kirstie gave the door one more shove. Her shoulder hurt from the impact, but it didn't shift. Then she, too, dropped to the floor.

And now the three men came running around the corner of the house, along the porch. Wes Logan burst out of the front door and joined them in the yard.

"Holy cow!" He swore as he saw the horse box shudder, caught sight of a tan horse backing down the ramp, hooves stamping and sparking on the metal surface. Crazy Horse backed free of the box and spun on the spot. He saw the men racing toward him. Back went his head, ears flat, teeth bared. He reared once, twice, three times, keeping them at bay.

Logan, Johnson, and Gibb shied away from the flailing hooves. The fourth man, several steps behind them, seemed to be the first to take in what was happening. "Stand clear!" he yelled as Crazy Horse jumped from the ramp. "The gray gelding broke loose! Get out of the way!"

"Great horse!" Kirstie breathed. "Good, good boy!"

Crazy Horse galloped in a tight circle around the yard. He rounded up three of the horse thieves as if they were cattle, backed them up against the fence. The fourth moved fast, made a run across the yard toward the tack room.

Then Cadillac stormed down the ramp, hooves thudding, nostrils flared. Freedom beckoned in the shape of his old friend, Crazy Horse. He broke out of the box into the yard, rearing and bucking, kicking up snow, squealing at the top of his voice.

"Let us out!" Kirstie thumped on the tack room door. She could see the legs and feet of the young, dark-haired accomplice through the crack. "Come on, unlock the door!"

Lying flat, staring at the booted feet, Lisa shook her head. "Save your breath," she muttered to Kirstie. "He's not about to risk his neck for us!"

The feet backed slowly toward the door while in the distance, Crazy Horse and Cadillac ran rings around Logan and his men. There was a click, the sound of a latch lifting and falling, then quickly, the feet moved away.

"Wrong!" Kirstie cried. She pushed at the door, and this time, it swung open.

Crazy Horse saw her in the doorway. He reared and turned, raced toward her. And as he approached, stirrups flying, feet pounding across the yard, a new sound threaded its way between the steep hills.

It was a high, two-toned, alien wailing sound. It grew louder, invaded the stands of aspen and pines, and echoed from cliff to cliff.

"Cops!" Johnson shouted. Logan and Gibb saw the flashing blue light reflected from the snow-covered banks of the valley. They darted behind Cadillac to raise the ramp and slam the bolts home. Then they made for the cab.

Crazy Horse skidded to a halt beside Kirstie. He wanted her in the saddle, working with him to save Cadillac. She hooked a foot into the stirrup, swung up and over. He wheeled and galloped back toward the three men.

Johnson was already in the cab, reaching out to haul Gibb up after him. Logan waited impatiently behind. With the truck engine running, the police-car sirens drew nearer, filling their heads, lights flashing bright blue against the snow.

And Crazy Horse charged straight at Wes Logan and the cab. Sent staggering away from the truck, winded, he doubled over, not knowing for a moment where he was or what had hit him.

Kirstie reined her horse to a halt by the fence, turned him, and charged again. No way was Logan going to escape.

Johnson sat at the wheel with Gibb at his side. Leaving their boss to his fate, he edged the truck forward to the exit onto the dirt road that ran along the valley bottom. San Luis Dawn squealed and cried out from her metal prison.

In the confusion, Logan tried to stand upright. But then he covered his head with both arms as Crazy Horse charged a second time.

The sirens wailed. Johnson revved the engine and drove like a maniac straight at the two patrol cars.

Inches from impact, he swerved the horse box to one side. The high vehicle swayed and skidded. Slowly, almost gracefully, it tilted and tipped. Inside, the horse squealed in terror.

And Kirstie felt Crazy Horse rear. She saw Logan sag and curl forward under his hooves, felt no pity as the horse surged through the air and brought his hooves driving down, down, down toward the cowering man.

**10**

"You could've killed the guy!" The deputy sheriff who'd hauled Wes Logan to safety was now busy clicking handcuffs shut around the ranch owner's wrists.

"But we didn't." Kirstie felt calm…almost empty, now that the sirens had stopped and cops were everywhere. "Crazy Horse knew what he was doing. We just wanted to stop Logan escaping, give him a scare."

"You sure did a good job." The young policeman wasn't gentle as he manhandled Logan toward the patrol car. "For the life of me, I thought the horse meant to trample the man to death!"

Kirstie stared down from the saddle. Logan didn't look so smooth or arrogant now. He was covered from head to foot in dirty snow, a scratch on his cheek trickled blood, and he hung his head as the cops bundled him into a car.

"Are you OK?" Lisa ran up and took Crazy Horse's rein. "Kirstie, talk to me. Are you OK?"

"We're fine." She blinked and pulled her attention around so as to convince her friend not to worry. "How about Cadillac?"

"Look over there." Lisa turned Crazy Horse around so that Kirstie faced the other way.

Matt and Sandy had stepped out of the second patrol car and walked slowly across the yard. They took in the scene: Logan and his two accomplices under arrest, Kirstie safe on Crazy Horse, Lisa standing nearby. And the lost white horse trotting to greet them.

Kirstie's brother stepped forward alone. He crossed the yard until he and Cadillac met in the middle. The horse lowered his graceful head. Matt reached out and touched him. Together again.

"Save the questions till later!" Matt had work to do. There was San Luis Dawn inside the overturned truck. The mare needed his attention before they could get her out.

Kirstie dismounted from Crazy Horse and followed him. "But how did you all get here? How come you knew we needed you?"

"Let Matt do his work," Sandy Scott said gently. She'd taken Cadillac's lead rope from her son and led the horse to one side as Matt climbed into the back of the truck. "How's she look?"

"She's spooked pretty bad. But she's on her feet, no bones broken. A couple of cuts on her front legs." Matt ran through the situation. "I'm gonna wait a while before I move in on her."

"So how come?" Kirstie turned her questions on her mom. "What happened with you?"

"Don't ask!" Sandy ran a hand through her hair and sighed. "Halfway down to the Falls, we get a call from Larry. He double-checks the tip-off, late as usual, because, deep down, he's not happy, and what does he find? The mystery caller's number has a San Luis code. He looks it up, traces it back here."

"To Ponderosa Pines?" Lisa broke in. She'd gone to get Lucky from his hiding place on the hillside and came in on the end of Sandy's explanation. "So Logan was the one who sent you on a wild goose chase?"

"Seems that way. Maybe he wanted to keep us busy while he trucked Cadillac out of here. Anyhow, by now, Larry definitely isn't smiling. He makes another call, this time to Columbine Falls. And guess what? The sale barn has no white gelding, three-quarters Thoroughbred for sale today!"

"Surprise!" Kirstie muttered. "So what did you do?"

"What could we do? We turn the car around and head for home. But we have a two-hour drive ahead of us, so we call Charlie at home to check in, tell him what's happening, and see how things are."

"And he tells you we've set out on the trail with Crazy Horse and Lucky!" Lisa predicted what was to come. "You go crazy with him for letting us out in a blizzard!"

Sandy grinned. "Something like that. Poor Charlie!"

"Hey, Mom!" Matt called from inside the horse box. "I need something to make a pressure pad, to stop the bleeding from one of these cuts!"

Lisa stepped in. "You wait here. I'll fetch bandages from the first-aid box in the tack room!"

"So things are falling into place." Sandy went on with her story, one ear open for more instructions from Matt. "Larry Francini is in the picture, and he's arranging to meet us at Half Moon Ranch to discuss what to do. Only Matt's worried about you and Lisa. He says we should head straight here in case you get yourselves into a fix."

"Talk about a sixth sense!" Kirstie's brother joked as he came to the buckled and dented back door of the horse box and reached out to take rolls of clean cotton bandage from a breathless Lisa.

"OK, so you know me!" Kirstie admitted grudgingly.

"Yeah, you and trouble, you're like magnets!" Matt disappeared back inside the horse box.

Sandy raised her eyebrows at Lisa but made no comment. "Meanwhile, Charlie calls us again. We're on Route 3, almost at San Luis by this time. Charlie says he just had a signal from the radio you'd taken along with you. The signal's all broken up, and he can't get a reply through to you. He's trying. He can hear Lisa's voice saying his name, sounding pretty scared, then suddenly the whole thing breaks up."

Kirstie nodded. "That was Johnson creeping up from behind in the stable. He smashed the radio before we could make contact."

"So now it's urgent." Sandy brought the girls up to date. "We get in touch with Larry again. He arranges for two cars to come straight over here and to meet up with us on the way…"

"And you made it!" Lisa concluded. "Boy, were we glad to see you!"

"But…!" Kirstie began. She saw the two patrol cars turn around in the narrow road. Logan sat in one, flanked by two cops. Gibb and Johnson had been bundled into the other. Alone in the yard, the young, dark-haired ranch hand who had set the girls free from the tack room watched from a safe distance.

"No buts!" Sandy cried. "Please, Kirstie, give us a break!"

"OK, I've strapped up the cut; we're coming out!" Matt called at last.

They stood back to give him and San Luis Dawn some space. And while they waited, Kirstie slipped away with Crazy Horse for answers to her final questions.

"So why Cadillac?" she asked their secret helper. "Why did your boss risk everything for the one horse?"

"To make a pair. Cadillac and San Luis Dawn came from the same stud. They're blood-related." He offered the explanation in a low voice, apologetic and embarrassed. "Mr. Logan fixed up a deal through his wife in California before he even put in an offer to your mom to buy Cadillac."

"And when she refused, he wasn't too happy?"

"He doesn't like being told 'no.' The way he looks at things, what he wants he gets. Legal or not."

"Did you know about the plan to steal Cadillac?" For some reason, this mattered a lot to Kirstie. "Were you the third rustler?"

"No. I wasn't in on it. Mr. Logan himself went along with Gibb and Johnson for the heist, I guess. Me, I'm just the drudge around here. They don't tell me a thing."

Kirstie took a deep breath. "Thanks for taking a risk and opening that door," she said quietly.

He gave her a fleeting grin before he turned and

went inside the stable to check on things in there. "No problem," he said. "Tell your brother I'm glad he got both his horses back."

Later that evening, when they were home at Half Moon Ranch, Kirstie passed on the message.

She sat with Matt on the fence overlooking Red Fox Meadow, legs dangling, hands in her jacket pockets.

"Not half as glad as I am," he said. His eyes followed Crazy Horse and Cadillac everywhere they went; feeding at the hayrack, trotting here and there amongst the herd of ranch horses just to let everyone know they were back.

Crazy Horse nosed up to Jitterbug and butted her in a friendly fashion. Cadillac danced up to Johnny Mohawk and shook his mane at him. Yukon and Moose wandered slowly by.

"Do we know how Crazy Horse got loose from Logan in the first place?" Matt was rerunning events from Sunday night to now.

"Rob says Gibb loaded him into the horse box, drove out onto Route 3, and dumped him," Kirstie answered. She smiled as Cadillac and

Crazy Horse spotted them on the fence and came toward them.

"'Rob says'!" Matt grinned from ear to ear.

"The young guy who let us out of the tack room," she explained, her face burning. Chalk it up to the evening sun hitting her as it sank behind Eagle's Peak. "He wasn't part of the robbery. He's staying put at Ponderosa Pines until they sort something out."

"Rob!" Matt wouldn't let it drop. "So how far does Rob say Gibb drove before he dumped Crazy Horse?"

Still blushing, determined to ignore Matt's teasing, Kirstie jumped into the meadow and went to meet the two horses. They approached in step, Cadillac adjusting his long stride to Crazy Horse's short legs. "Thirty or forty miles," she told him. "A heck of a long walk back here!"

"What a star!" Matt followed her into the meadow. As Kirstie walked toward Cadillac, he split off and met the sturdy, plain, ordinary quarter horse with the strong, loyal heart. He slung an arm around his neck and walked with him.

"How many people do you know who would

do as much for a friend?" Kirstie asked. Cadillac lowered his head to nuzzle her shoulder, keeping Crazy Horse at the edge of his sight.

"Not many. Animals, yes. People, no." Matt fell into step with the geldings. "Animals give you loyalty, no question."

"Especially horses," Kirstie murmured happily. "Though I'd do it for Lisa, I guess."

"Risk your life?" Matt mused.

Holding up her wrist to show him her bracelet, Kirstie nodded. They walked in silence toward the sun.

"Mom's happy," Matt said out of nowhere.

"That's good." Kirstie stopped, one hand on Cadillac's neck.

"We talked. I'm gonna finish college, be a vet."

She took a deep, deep breath. "That's real good."

Crazy Horse leaned his head across Matt to nudge her arm. His mane fell across his half-closed eyes, he seemed to be smiling: *It's been a close call, but hey, everything worked out fine!*

**THE HORSES OF HALF MOON RANCH**

## WILD HORSES

Kirstie is leading a horse trek through Miners' Ridge when a sudden storm causes a landslide. She is trapped alone in Dead Man's Canyon with a herd of wild horses whose leader—a proud stallion—has been hurt by falling rocks. Cold, wet, and alone in the gathering storm—can she find a way out and help the injured stallion?

# RODEO ROCKY

While at a local rodeo contest, Kirstie is horrified to see how Rocky, an injured horse, is treated. Kirstie persuades her mother to buy him but soon learns that training an ex-rodeo horse is not easy. And when Rocky throws Kirstie on a trail far from the ranch, she quickly realizes that the only way to get them both home safely is to trust herself and the unruly horse.

# JOHNNY MOHAWK

Kirstie Scott knows her beloved horses are friendly and gentle, so when a guest at Half Moon Ranch
accuses Johnny Mohawk of throwing him off, she
is positive that he is lying. With the threat of a
lawsuit looming, Kirstie must prove that Johnny
Mohawk is not to blame before time runs
out. Kirstie is certainly no detective, so how
can she possibly prove that Johnny Mohawk is
truly innocent?

## MIDNIGHT LADY

Kirstie Scott can't wait to meet the neighbors that have just moved in, especially their strong-willed and elegant mare, Midnight Lady. But she is shocked to discover that they mistreat their horses. Appalled by the abuse, she vows to rescue them. However, her plan backfires when many of the horses escape deep into the mountains. Kirstie is now faced with a tough choice—confess or sneak off herself in search of Midnight Lady and the other missing horses.

## THIRD-TIME LUCKY

Kirstie Scott adores all of her horses, but Lucky is her favorite. She is devastated when Lucky suddenly falls ill and his life hangs in the balance. Even more unsettling is that no one can figure out what's wrong with him. Desperate for answers, Kirstie takes Lucky deep into the Rockies to find a reclusive but legendary horse doctor before she loses her beloved friend. Who is this mysterious doctor—and will he even be able to save Lucky?

# ABOUT THE AUTHOR

Born and brought up in Harrogate, Yorkshire, Jenny Oldfield went on to study English at Birmingham University, where she did research on the Brontë novels and on children's literature. She then worked as a teacher before deciding to concentrate on writing. She writes novels for both children and adults and, when she can escape from her desk, likes to spend time outdoors. She loves the countryside and enjoys walking, gardening, playing tennis, riding, and traveling with her two daughters, Kate and Eve.